"You said we could talk. Are you going to let me in or not?"

"Not on your life!" Blair choked. How dare he think he had only to smile that crooked grin and she would greet him with open arms! "Go away, Cameron. My office hours are eight-thirty to five. Come back then."

"Are you sure?" he murmured huskily. His hand began a slow, seductive climb, moving up her arm to her shoulder before coming to rest on her neck, his thumb teasing the pulse that fluttered there.

She stared at him, unable to break the invisible bond that stretched between them. A sweet tide of half-forgotten longing swept over her, and without conscious thought, she melted against him.

"Are you sure you don't want me?" he whispered.

Her body welcomed his touch, gloried in it. She closed her eyes against the intense pleasure his fingers evoked and was shocked at the low moan that erupted from her throat. God, she had missed him!

"We never had any problems in bed, did we?" he growled...

Dear Reader:

Romance readers today have more choice among books than ever before. But with so many titles to choose from, deciding what to select becomes increasingly difficult.

At SECOND CHANCE AT LOVE we try to make that decision easy for you — by publishing romances of the highest quality every month. You can confidently buy any SECOND CHANCE AT LOVE romance and know it will provide you with solid romantic entertainment.

Sometimes you buy romances by authors whose work you've previously read and enjoyed — which makes a lot of sense. You're being sensible... and careful... to look for satisfaction where you've found it before.

But if you're *too* careful, you risk overlooking exceptional romances by writers whose names you don't immediately recognize. These first-time authors may be the stars of tomorrow, and you won't want to miss any of their books! At SECOND CHANCE AT LOVE, many writers who were once "new" are now the most popular contributors to the line. So trying a new writer at SECOND CHANCE AT LOVE isn't really a risk at all. Every book we publish must meet our rigorous standards — whether it's by a popular "regular" or a newcomer.

In the months to come, we urge you to watch for these names — Linda Raye, Karen Keast, Betsy Osborne, Dana Daniels, and Cinda Richards. All are dazzling new writers, an elite few whose books are destined to become "keepers." We think you'll be delighted and excited by their first books with us!

Look, too, for romances by writers with whom you're already warmly familiar: Jeanne Grant, Ann Cristy, Linda Barlow, Elissa Curry, Jan Mathews, and Liz Grady, among many others.

Best wishes,

Ellen Edwards

Ellen Edwards, Senior Editor
SECOND CHANCE AT LOVE
The Berkley Publishing Group
200 Madison Avenue
New York, N.Y. 10016

MADE IN HEAVEN

LINDA RAYE

A SECOND CHANCE AT LOVE BOOK

MADE IN HEAVEN

Copyright © 1984 by Linda Ray Turner

All rights reserved. No part of this publication may be reproduced or transmitted in any form or by any means, electronic or mechanical, including photocopy, recording, or any information storage and retrieval system, without permission in writing from the publisher.

Requests for permission to make copies of any part of the work should be mailed to: Permissions, Second Chance at Love, The Berkley Publishing Group, 200 Madison Avenue, New York, NY 10016.

First edition published October 1984

First printing

"Second Chance at Love" and the butterfly emblem are trademarks belonging to Jove Publications, Inc.

Printed in the United States of America

Second Chance at Love books are published by
The Berkley Publishing Group
200 Madison Avenue, New York, NY 10016

- 1 -

THE NINETEENTH-CENTURY GRANDFATHER clock struck the half hour, its heavy, sonorous tones elegantly shattering the quiet of the apartment. In the kitchen Blair Wakefield's slim fingers abandoned their task of measuring spices into the food processor to push back stray wisps of sandy hair from her temples. Unconsciously she stiffened, nervously clutching the folds of the mustard-colored apron tied around her small waist.

Impending doom. It stood behind her; she could feel it waiting, watching, just as it had all day. What was the matter with her? She had no reason to feel apprehensive. In the past two years she'd hosted hundreds of parties. This one was no different than any of the others.

Liar, a voice scoffed. She wasn't fooling anyone, least of all herself. Tonight's little soiree was no ordinary gathering. Boston's best, the cream of the old Brahmin families, would soon be walking through the front door. Two years ago that thought would have terrified her, but then she had been struggling to be one of them, eager for their approval and acceptance. Now, when it no longer mattered, she was actually looking forward to the confrontation.

A thoughtful frown spread from her gold-flecked green eyes to the delicate lines of her face, casting a shadow over high cheekbones, a pert nose, and a mouth that was just now learning to smile again. Fleeting memories clouded her mind, and as she removed the curried cheese pâté from the refrigerator and headed for the library, the warm beige tones of the luxurious apartment gave way to the past. Waltz evenings at the Copley Plaza, Friday-afternoon symphony concerts, painfully uncomfortable forays into Boston society.

She winced. How gauche she had been then. Scarcely an adult at the time, she had left the security of her parents' home for the wealth and glitter of her husband's. She had always felt like an outsider, a feeling she could now attribute to her own insecurities and immaturity. In the beginning she hadn't known the first thing about society, and fear had glued her to her husband's side. He had come to hate those occasions as much as she.

Those days were gone, however, and with them her innocent naiveté, her fear, her husband. Now she could handle practically anything.

You've come a long way, baby, she told herself proudly, remembering those awful days after the divorce when things couldn't have looked bleaker. She had only been twenty-one, responsible for her two-year-old daughter, unemployed, and unskilled in anything but the wifely duties, the proper performance of which had been instilled in her from childhood. It was that proficiency that she turned into her biggest asset by establishing a rent-a-wife service that provided bachelors with the cooking, cleaning, and managing skills found only in wives. In a town full of eligible bachelors she had filled a void, her success guaranteed. Now, after two years, she administered the business, leaving the actual work to the four women who assisted her. However, she still found time to work with special clients, such as Stan.

The slamming of the front door jolted her back to the

present. She laid the pâté on the bar and hurried to the foyer, whisking off the apron that protected her jeans and beige sweater. Stan Harper, his red hair practically standing on end from his habit of running his fingers through it, turned at her entrance, an odd mixture of anxiety and relief written on his square-jawed face. "Blair! Thank God, you're here!"

"Of course I'm here." She laughed in confusion, helping him with his khaki overcoat, which he hadn't bothered to button. "Where else would I be? I've got a hundred things left to do in the next thirty minutes, including getting dressed." Tossing him his coat, she turned back toward the kitchen, casting him a teasing grin over her shoulder. "Don't worry, Stan, everything will be ready. I've waited two years for this night, two years to prove to myself that I can hold my own with this crowd. Tonight I'm going to knock their socks off! Wait'll you see my dress."

"I'm not worried about you," he denied, following her into the kitchen. "I mean, I am, but it has nothing to do with the party. Blair, I've got to talk to you."

"Not now. The guests will be here any minute and I still haven't restocked the bar or lit the candles. Damn! I forgot about ice." She started for the door. "And you have to change, too."

"But. . . ."

She frowned when she saw he hadn't moved. "Hurry up, Stan, or you're going to be late for your own party." Before he could protest further, she swept into the library to deposit an artfully arranged vegetable tray next to the pâté.

Poor Stan. He was such a worrier. And it was all so unnecessary. She had everything under control. The apartment was spotless, with flowers and candles ready to add bright Christmas cheer. And the food was excellent, as good or better than anything prepared by the guests' private chefs and caterers.

In the guest room she threw off her jeans and sweater and slipped into the mint-green dress she had laid out when she first arrived at the apartment. How she loved that dress! The cool silk slid over her body to envelop her in a cloud of almost sinful softness, bringing a sigh of pleasure. There was no question about it; the dress was made for her. Like a misty glen, the cool green matched her eyes to perfection, the wispy, almost transparent material clinging to her small breasts and waist, coyly revealing everything but what the silk underslip concealed. And with each step she felt like a dream in motion, the full skirt playfully swirling about her legs.

The mirror told her what she had suspected: she had never looked better. The last two years had taken their toll, chiseling away at the extra pounds she had retained after pregnancy until she was slimmer than she'd been when she married. Excitement added an extra glow to her cheeks and eyes, a sparkle that hadn't been there for a very long time. She swept her tawny curls up off her neck and grinned triumphantly as the disarrayed mass fell back to her shoulders seductively. Tonight she was ready for anything.

With a final dab of perfume to the low neckline of her dress, she returned to the library for one last critical check of her surroundings. She loved this room. From carpet to ceiling it was awash in earthy sand tones. Red candles and poinsettias provided bright splashes of fire along with the scarlet silk throw pillows tossed carelessly but effectively on the cream-colored couch. Stan's apartment occupied the entire corner of the apartment tower, and the wide windows offered a breathtaking view of the Charles River as well as downtown Boston.

"Blair, I know you're busy, but I've got to talk to you now." Still buttoning the blue silk shirt she had bought him only yesterday, Stan strode purposefully into the library.

In an amazingly short time he had showered and changed and even managed to make his rebelliously curly red hair behave. For once his brown eyes had lost their twinkle. Blair had the sinking feeling he was about to tell her something she did not want to hear. "There's really no time—" she began.

"It's about Cameron."

Her heart contracted, her eyes closing in an instinctive effort to shut Cameron Wakefield out of her life once and for all. He meant nothing to her, she told herself firmly.

Made in Heaven

He hadn't for a very long time now. He was only a name from her past. An old lover. An old husband. Discarded by mutual agreement. The only emotion his name conjured up was a pain better left forgotten.

"Is he hurt? Sick?" The words slipped out, faint but nevertheless audible. She had to ask.

"He's sick, all right," Stan retorted bitterly. "Sick in the head. I—"

The ringing of the doorbell sliced rudely through his words. "Damn!" he exclaimed impatiently. "I'll get that."

Blair grabbed his arm when he started to move past her. "Wait a minute. You can't drop a bomb like that and just walk away. What about Cameron?"

"I'll tell you later."

The next few moments were filled with greetings, for once the doorbell rang, it seemed to continue nonstop for the next forty minutes. Blair watched Stan perform the role of charming, sophisticated host and could have cheerfully kicked him. Instead she pasted a smile on her face and jumped into her role as hostess, circulating, making sure there was plenty of food and drink.

She knew most of the guests; she had socialized with them many times during her marriage. Stan's parents, business associates, family friends—they were all there. Although a few people expressed surprise upon seeing her, her presence in their midst after a two-year absence raised relatively few eyebrows. In fact, everyone was relaxed and enjoying themselves. She had no fears about the food; it was the hit of the party. So why was she still so apprehensive?

She stepped out of the kitchen with another tray of stuffed mushrooms and came face-to-face with Mary Whitaker, Cameron's godmother. Blair paled in spite of her best efforts to appear nonchalant. Of all his friends and family, this woman she had liked the most. She hadn't seen her since the divorce. Would she blame her, just as all the Wakefields had?

The older woman studied Blair openly. "It's been a long time. You've changed."

Blair smiled, choosing to take the woman's words as a compliment. "Yes, I have. I like to think it's for the better."

"If the rumors I've heard are true, it's definitely for the better. Did you put this party together?"

"Yes."

Mary Whitaker shook her graying head in disgust. "Cameron was a fool to let you get away. And he didn't like it one bit when I told him so." She locked eyes with Blair. "Have you seen him? How is he?"

Blair stiffened. She didn't want to discuss Cameron; she didn't even want to think about him. For reasons she refused to analyze, it was just too painful. "I really don't know how he is, Mary. I haven't seen him recently."

Blair hadn't seen Cameron for two years, in fact—not since he moved to London. The few times he did get back to Boston to see Julie, she had made it a point to be out. She wouldn't, couldn't, see him. Julie was the only bond between them now, and Cameron made sure their letters and phone calls were strictly limited to their daughter's welfare. He wasn't at all interested in Blair's personal life, which wasn't too surprising, considering the circumstances under which they had parted.

Something had snapped in both of them that day. She had accused him of being just like his father—living for his career, with his wife and family of only secondary importance.

He, in turn, wanted nothing to do with what he considered her childish dreams of a fairy-tale, happily-ever-after love. He moved to London without her, and a part of her died in the process. Even now she sometimes hurt in the still of the night.

Determinedly she threw herself into the spirit of the party, bandying with ease the questions and curiosity about Maid-In-Heaven. She knew that parties such as this one were better than the best advertising for the rent-a-wife service. Two years of hard work in establishing the business had paid off: Maid-In-Heaven had already begun to make quite a name for itself. And now Stan, bless his heart, was making sure she met every single new, prospective client. Tomorrow the phone would be ringing off the wall.

An hour passed, and then another. Blair retreated to the kitchen and placed another bowl of seafood pilaf in the microwave to heat, smiling in satisfaction at the hum of conversation and laughter drifting into the kitchen from the library. Everything was going so well....

Suddenly two arms snaked around her from behind to enfold her in a fierce hug. She gasped and glanced over her shoulder to find Stan grinning at her boyishly. She laughed.

"Stan, you idiot! What are you doing?"

"I'm thanking you for a fabulous party. Who else but you would have thought of seafood for a Christmas party? It was a terrific idea."

She grinned, pleased by the compliment. "You'd better watch your flattery. My rates may go up."

"You're costing me an arm and a leg now. I might as well get my money's worth." He grabbed her wrist and pulled her out of the kitchen, his eyes alight with laughter. "You haven't danced all evening."

"But, Stan...the food..."

Her feeble protest was drowned out by the music. Someone had turned off the stereo, and Peter Walker, the sports editor of the Boston *Tribune*, was banging out a wild boogie-woogie on the piano while the younger members of the crowd tried to jitterbug. Blair felt the music grab her and longed to join in the fun, but she couldn't completely forget her responsibilities as hostess. When Stan pulled her among the dancing couples, she warned, "You're going to have a lot of hungry people on your hands if you don't let me check the food."

"They won't starve. Right now you're going to have a little fun. And that's an order from the boss." Before she could protest again, he hugged her around the waist and stepped into a crazy rendition of the forties-style dance, which she had no choice but to follow.

Blair found herself giggling and matching her steps with Stan's, her dress billowing about her as he took her hand and twirled her around in front of him. The old swing music was timeless. They were surrounded by laughing, happy faces, and Blair had the satisfaction of knowing she had contributed to the party's success. She willingly forgot about the food and decided to enjoy herself. She did love to dance, and she hadn't done it for so long. Not since Cameron....

Cameron! The room suddenly tilted at a crazy angle as Blair's eyes were drawn across a sea of faces to one that towered over all the rest. Her heart dropped to her feet in a dizzy rush, draining her face of color before surging back up to her throat to rob her of breath. She clutched at Stan, her fingers biting into his arm, and found it impossible to drag her eyes away from the man who had once held her heart in his hands. Cameron. He was there, at the party, the physical manifestation of a dream that had once haunted her.

In a roomful of beautiful people he stood out. The wind had tossed his teak-colored hair into boyish disarray, sweeping the dark locks down into coal-black eyes that gleamed with an inner light. His teeth flashed in a smile as he turned to say something to one of the guests who greeted him, igniting an ache in Blair that she couldn't ignore. How well she knew that smile. Invariably it started in his eyes and spread slowly to his mouth, warming the sometimes harsh lines of his face and somehow making the person on the receiving end of that smile feel very special.

How many times had she traced his features in the dark with her fingers, her mouth? The hard cut of his cheekbones, the wide, intelligent forehead, and the thick brows that could lower threateningly or quirk in amusement—she knew them as well as she knew the rest of his tall, lean body: intimately. Once, love had softened the arrogant set of his mouth and tempered a granite jaw that could be unbearably tenacious and uncompromising. But that was long ago. She had discovered that, without love, he could look through her blankly, indifferently.

She drew in a ragged breath that seared her suddenly tight throat. *Impending doom!* This was it. Hadn't she known all day that disaster was at hand? It had been a gut feeling that refused to go away, choosing instead to linger in the crevices of her subconscious until it could be personified in the six-foot-plus frame of her ex-husband.

He was magnificent, she thought as he shrugged out of his black topcoat. But then, he had always looked wonderful in evening clothes. The ebony jacket hugged his broad shoulders in elegant contrast to his snow-white studded shirt. He was the epitome of what every man should look like in a tux, but few did. And the pull his body had on her heartstrings terrified her. She wanted to stand before him and feel absolutely nothing, but she couldn't, dammit! He stirred her senses even though she fought the attraction with every ounce of strength she possessed.

He wasn't surprised to see her. As soon as he had entered the room his opaque eyes had scanned the crowd and found her. He spoke to friends absently, indifferently. His complete attention was focused on her face. Like a hunter stalking game, his gaze never left her face. He threaded his way through the crowd with a single-mindedness that left Blair mesmerized in Stan's hold.

She felt a trap closing in around her and could do nothing to stop it. She wanted to run, to hide, to escape those intense eyes. The hateful words and recriminations had all been uttered in another lifetime. She couldn't endure it again.

Desperately Blair searched for the strength to face this man she had once adored. The confidence she had worked so hard to develop over the past two lonely years was outraged by her sudden weakness. Cameron Wakefield meant less to her than a stranger on the street. She had no need to fear him. It was her own racing heart she feared.

The arm around her waist stiffened, and Blair looked up in surprise. Stan... she had forgotten him. Now she could see that she was not the only one affected by Cameron's appearance. Stan's lighthearted mood had vanished. In its stead was wariness and an antagonism that Blair was at odds to explain. When he noticed her puzzled frown, his arm around her tightened reassuringly. "I tried to tell you, Blair, but you wouldn't let me. I never dreamed he'd show up at the party."

If only she had known. She could have prepared herself for a meeting with him. Instead her thoughts were in a jumble, her defenses scattered. She could only try to greet him with as much reserve as she could muster and pray he wouldn't hear the pounding of her heart.

Despite her resolve, she was unprepared for his first words. "I believe this is our dance."

"Dance?" she choked. "Are you crazy? What are you doing here?"

"Looking for you, of course," he replied with a grin, his black eyes suddenly gleaming with devilish lights, daring her. He held out his hand. "Are you going to dance or not?"

"Dammit, Cameron!" Stan hissed, glancing around at the guests avidly watching the scene unfolding before them. "What the hell do you think you're doing? If you think I'm going to stand by and let you cause a scene..."

"I'm not the one causing the scene," Cameron pointed out innocently before turning his attention back to Blair, a craggy brow cocked challengingly, only the hint of a smile playing about his mouth. "Well?"

What was he up to? Blair wondered wildly, searching his face frantically for a clue to what was going on behind his dancing eyes. But his thoughts were shuttered behind a charming smile that dared her to put aside her doubts and take a chance. She couldn't resist him when he was in a mischievous mood, and he knew it. But she couldn't just walk into his arms even though her heart wasted no time in placing her hand in his. She hung back. "Cameron..."

"Dance with the poor boy," Mary Whitaker ordered gruffly as she came up to take Stan's other arm. "One dance isn't going to hurt. Anyway, Stan's been avoiding me all night. It's time he did his duty as host and danced with an old woman."

Cameron chuckled at Stan's impatient frown and pulled Blair closer to his side. "You're not an old woman, Mary, you're an angel."

"And you owe me one," she replied pertly. "Just make sure you don't blow this chance."

"Don't worry. I don't intend to," he assured her. He turned to Blair and opened his arms.

Blair was caught up in a dream; it never entered her head

to protest. Automatically she adjusted her steps to his, and her head found the spot on his shoulder that had always been hers. His warmth engulfed her, heating her blood, assailing her senses, and she was so overwhelmed by poignant memories that she was unable to pay any heed to the warnings her head was screaming at her heart. But when the music glided smoothly into "Weekend in New England," her heart tripped and fell out of the past, pain tearing at her. Suddenly chilled to the bone, she struggled to put some space between them. Pulling back as far as his arms would allow, she glared at him resentfully. "Did you bribe Peter to play that?"

The smile faded from his eyes. "No. I didn't realize memories of our honeymoon were so painful for you."

"They aren't," she replied. "They just remind me that there's no such thing as 'happily ever after.'" An aching emptiness spread through her body, an emptiness so pervasive that even when she looked at the crowd surrounding them—the elegant clothes, the laughter—she felt nothing. Those awful days after the divorce had been the bleakest days of her life; never again would she let anyone hurt her that badly. Almost imperceptibly the barriers protecting her battered heart dropped smoothly into place. Her eyes turned back to his. "How did you know I was here?"

"I went to the house. Your mother and Julie told me you were here." His mouth tightened into a grimace of distaste. "When did you start working for 'Uncle' Stan?"

"What is this, an inquisition?" she asked lightly, although indignation threatened to choke her. He had no right to question her about anything.

"Just idle curiosity," he admitted with a rueful grin that was belied by the gleam in his black eyes. "You know me. When I smell a story, I go after it." He dipped his head as if to inhale the perfumed fragrance of her hair. "When we were married, you used to hate this type of thing," he whispered in her ear. "Or did you just hate going with me?"

His breath warmed her sensitive skin, delighting her, torturing her with a sweet flood of memories. She groaned inwardly and tried to hold on to reality. "It had nothing to do with you. It was me. I was insecure." God, would this song never end? The touch of his hand on her back, of his thighs brushing hers, was driving her crazy, awakening sleeping desires, needs, that couldn't possibly be assuaged. She wanted so desperately to remain cool and unaffected by his closeness, but her body refused to cooperate. She had to put some distance between them before she made a fool of herself. "Cameron, why are you here? If you wanted to let me know you were in town, you could have left a message with my mother—though I can't imagine why you'd want to see me. We have nothing to say to each other."

"Do you find it so impossible to believe that I might have wanted to see you? To touch you?" he growled softly. His hand moved down her spine, igniting a fire in the pit of her stomach, weakening her knees. "I had to come back, honey. I couldn't stay away any longer. What we had was too good to throw away."

Blair's heart lurched painfully in her breast, her stunned eyes locking with his. "No."

"Yes. We've got to talk. I'm tired of living alone, sleeping alone. Somehow we got off on the wrong track—"

"You'll have to save this for later, Cameron," Stan cut in smoothly, arriving at their side just as the music ended. "Blair's working. If she wants to talk to you—which I seriously doubt—she can do it on her own time, not mine."

Cameron shot him an impatient glance before again fixing his gaze on Blair. "Mind your own business, Stan. This is between me and Blair. Keep your nose out of it."

"Stop it! Both of you!" Blair hissed, cringing from the curious eyes that were trained on them. What was wrong with these two? They were best friends, closer than some brothers, yet they were squared off like two adversaries, each waiting for the other to make the first move. She stared at them in confusion. "I don't know what's wrong between you two, but if you don't stop this right now—"

"Don't come in here and start trying to throw your weight around, Cameron," Stan ground out, ignoring Blair. "You weren't even invited to this party, so you're already treading on thin ice. Don't push your luck!"

"Would you like me to leave?"

"Yes...no!" Stan sputtered, the quiet question catching him off guard. He swore softly. "Dammit, I don't care if you stay. Just don't cause any trouble."

Cameron's eyebrows shot up, unexpected amusement sparkling in his eyes. *"Moi?* I just came to see my wife."

"Your ex-wife," Stan reminded him swiftly. "You're divorced. Remember?"

The amusement disappeared from Cameron's face as quickly as it had appeared. "It's not something I'm likely to forget," he retorted flatly. "Especially when I find her in another man's arms." His eyes snared Blair's. "I thought you were supposed to be working," he said disapprovingly, "not dancing. Just what kind of work are you doing?"

"Something I'm good at," she snapped. How dare he question her! "The fate of the world may not hinge on it, but a lot of bachelors appreciate my services. If you want a better explanation than that, you can come to the office. I'll give you a brochure. Now, if you'll excuse me, I've got work to do."

She fled into the kitchen without a backward glance, practically shaking as a delayed reaction swept over her. On the rare occasions when she had pictured an eventual meeting with Cameron, her fantasy had been nothing like the reality of tonight. The memories that stood between them were abysmal. Oh, the wounds they had inflicted on each other had healed, but the scars were there and still tender. They would always be tender. Would she ever be able to look at him without remembering the strength of his arms around her?

Agitation soon pulled her back into the living room, her eyes scanning the crowd to catch sight of Cameron standing at the piano, talking to Peter Walker. She and Peter were old friends, and when Cameron laughed, she consciously had to quell the urge to walk to his side and have him warm the coldness that gripped her heart. She started to turn away, but his eyes caught hers, and in that instant she knew that he was waiting. But for what? Her?

She shivered and turned quickly away, almost running into Stan in the process. She stopped short, all her frustrations, her confusion, spilling forth. "Dammit, Stan, what's going on? What's Cameron doing here? And why were you deliberately trying to antagonize him?"

"Antagonize *him?*" Stan exclaimed indignantly. "Where have you been? In case you didn't notice, he gave as good as he got." He ran his fingers through his hair, his eyes suddenly defensive. "Believe it or not, I was only trying to protect you. Any normal girl would have wanted me to stand up for her."

"In the first place I'm a woman, not a girl. And I can fight my own battles, thank you." She sighed, the anger suddenly draining out of her. "I don't understand you two. You were worse than two dogs fighting over a bone. And I was the bone!"

"This has nothing to do with you." He looked over her shoulder to see one of his father's business associates heading for him, and swore under his breath. "We can't talk now. I'll try to explain everything after the party."

Seeing she had little choice in the matter, Blair nodded and watched him walk away. She longed to escape to the kitchen, to forget her own reaction to Cameron's sudden appearance. But she knew from past experience that hiding would accomplish nothing. She turned to find Mary Whitaker at her side. "I suppose you heard," Blair said.

"Enough." The older woman's rather stern features softened, her brown eyes suddenly dancing as they lighted on Cameron's tall figure across the room. "There's hope for that boy yet."

Blair frowned. "Don't get any ideas, Mary. Cameron made his choice two years ago. It's over between us. Don't you dare try to play matchmaker."

"Would I do that?" she asked innocently. "You and Cameron have to solve your problems by yourself. Just don't be fooled by that cloak of ambition he protects himself with. He wants a home and family just as much as you do. Give him time. He'll come around to your way of thinking."

More disturbed by Mary's words than she cared to admit,

Blair forced herself to continue in the role of hostess. But for the first time since she started Maid-In-Heaven, she didn't enjoy her work. She was constantly aware of Cameron's eyes on her, following her, caressing her. He did nothing to interfere with her work, yet he was a constant distraction. When he finally left, wishing her good night before taking his leave, she was miserable. Where was he going? Would she see him again before he returned to London? Did she want to see him again? The endless questions bombarded her, but somehow she was able to lift her chin and pretend she wasn't going quietly out of her mind.

Everyone left... finally. By the time Stan closed the door on the last guest, Blair's head was splitting. After Cameron's departure, everyone had been painfully polite, but the party had been ruined for Blair. It was one of the worst evenings of her life. When Stan returned to the library after seeing the last guests out, she was in no mood for levity or tact. "All right, Stan, let's have it. Just what do you think you were doing tonight?"

"Don't you think you're asking the wrong person?" he demanded indignantly. "I wasn't the one who crashed the party and questioned your business practices."

She rubbed the tense muscles at the back of her neck. "I don't know why I'm blaming all this on you," she said tiredly. "Cameron was the one who barged in, thinking God knows what...."

Stan eyed her shrewdly. "Why should you care what Cameron thinks? You divorced him."

She sank onto the couch. Yes, she had divorced him. It had been the most difficult decision of her life, but she'd really had no choice. She and Cameron had wanted two different things out of marriage, and their goals just weren't compatible. She wanted a husband who was devoted to keeping their marriage and family together. She had to come first with him, just as he came first with her. With Cameron she never did. He wanted success. That came before marriage, family, love. During the first year of their marriage, she was uneasy with the time he devoted to his career, jealous of the time it took him away from her. His parents' marriage was always there as a shining example, proof positive that two people could lead completely separate lives, meeting only in the bedroom. She didn't want that with Cameron. She had fought it for three years, but when he accepted the job in London without even discussing it with her, she saw the writing on the wall.

"I don't care what he thinks of me personally," she explained, ignoring Stan's knowing look, "but I won't let him belittle Maid-In-Heaven. I've worked hard establishing that business, and I'm not going to stand back and let Cameron question it. Doesn't he know there's more to arranging a party than calling a caterer?"

"He was just jealous," Stan replied. "His ego probably took quite a beating when he discovered you weren't pining away for him." He perched on a bar stool, his face suddenly bleak. "Damn! This has been a hell of a day!"

Blair eyed him thoughtfully, noting the rigidity of his shoulders, the angry clenching of his fingers. "What's happened between you and Cameron?" she asked softly. "And don't try to put me off by saying Cameron was jealous. It goes much deeper than that."

For a moment she didn't think he was going to answer. But suddenly the anger crumbled, and for the first time he allowed her to see the hurt and confusion that gripped him. "He resigned today."

"Resigned!" Blair stared at him, stunned. Frantic thoughts tripped over each other. Cameron had resigned as the London-based foreign correspondent for Harper Publications, an international media network. Stan's father was founder and chairman of the board, but he had never shown the slightest favoritism toward his son or his son's best friend. Like Terrence Harper, Stan and Cameron had joined the Boston *Tribune* right out of college and learned the newspaper business from the ground up. She couldn't remember the number of anniversaries, birthdays, and dinners Cameron had missed in his effort to forge a career with Harper Publications. In the end he left their marriage to accept the London job. Now he had quit. Two years too late. How ironic.

Made in Heaven 17

"It's hard to believe, isn't it?" Stan remarked gruffly. "I was floored. He just walked in today and resigned. No notice, no nothing. There was no reasoning with him. He had made up his mind before he even walked in the door."

"But why? He had to give a reason, Stan. No one quits after nine years without a very good reason."

"He bought the *Gazette*."

"The *Gazette*? But I thought it was folding."

"It would have if Cameron had let it die a natural death. He's convinced the paper's main problem is management. Personally I think he's going to get a kick out of stealing business from my father."

"Oh, come on, Stan. You can't honestly believe that," she objected. "You're taking this too personally. Even if Cameron does succeed with the *Gazette*, he can't possibly hurt your father's business. Harper Publications is too big."

"Maybe not, but it hasn't done a hell of a lot for our friendship. Do you know he's caused a major shake-up at the *Tribune*? Jack Trawick's leaving to be in charge of advertising. He knows everybody in town, and he won't hesitate to call in a few favors owed him. Do you have any idea what that can do to our revenue?" Resentment hardened his eyes. "No, he's out for blood. Valerie Roland's going to be his new city editor."

Realization hit Blair like a ton of bricks. Stan was jealous! Valerie Roland had joined the *Tribune* staff four months earlier and had instantly attracted the attention of every male in sight, including Stan. Tall, beautiful, and intelligent, Valerie knew what she wanted and went after it. She had made no secret of the fact that she wanted Stan. He, unfortunately, had fallen hard for another woman with similar attributes less than a year earlier, only to discover that the woman had hoped to use him, the owner's son, to gain the first rung on the ladder of success. The more persistent Valerie became, the more she convinced Stan she was trying to use him. And now Cameron had stolen her right out from under his nose.

Blair bit back a smile. "What are you going to do about it? Let her walk away without even lifting a finger?"

"What am I supposed to do?" he asked in exasperation. "The woman's got ink in her veins. She doesn't even want more money. She's got some crazy idea of being another Pulitzer or something. Cameron's promised her the excitement of building a paper from the ashes. How can I compete with that?"

"There must be something..."

He shook his head and started stacking the dirty dishes that littered the bar. "I should have expected this. Valerie's too ambitious to stay in one place for long. She's the best damn reporter I've got, but she's aiming for the top, and she'll use any means to get there. She used the *Tribune* as a stepping-stone just like Cameron did."

"You know Cameron has always dreamed of owning his own paper, Stan," she objected, automatically coming to Cameron's defense. "He's dedicated his life to the newspaper business, turning his back on Wakefield Electronics and a vice-presidency, fighting his family every step of the way. This is the chance of a lifetime, and you can't blame him for jumping at it."

"I certainly didn't expect him to go into business right here in Boston. My father was furious when Cameron told him he bought the *Gazette*."

Blair picked up the nearly empty food platters and followed Stan into the kitchen. She wasn't thrilled about Cameron's plans either, although her reasons were entirely different. After all this time he was poised to reenter her life. From now on she would never know when she would turn around and stumble over him.

"I guess that leaves you in the middle," Stan said.

Blair blinked. "What?"

"Cameron and I are on opposite sides of the fence," he explained patiently. "And right now you're straddling it. I wouldn't blame you if you wanted to drop me as a client."

"Drop you?" She whirled to face him, alarm widening her eyes. "Don't be ridiculous. You were my first client! And as for Cameron, I'm no longer a part of his life."

"You'll always be a part of his life. You're the mother of his daughter," he reminded her gently. "And in case you didn't notice, he was more than a little jealous when he found you dancing with me. You might as well face it, Blair, you'll probably be seeing a lot of Cameron from now on."

"Seeing a lot of him?" She was beginning to sound like a parrot, she thought in irritation. "Why would I see Cameron? I don't want to have anything to do with him."

"And what about Julie? Do you expect her to avoid him, too?" His hands settled on her shoulders. "Blair, you're going to have to accept it, like it or not. One of his reasons for returning to Boston was to be closer to Julie. He hasn't seen much of her in the last two years. Believe me, he's going to make up for it, now that he's home."

"I don't care. He can see Julie; I want him to see her. She's been without a father for too long. But that has nothing to do with me." She stomped into the library, sudden anger flooding her. "I won't let Cameron disrupt my life again. Or interfere. I'm running my own business and loving every minute of it. Cameron's return to Boston has nothing to do with that. He has no rights where I'm concerned. He gave that up years ago."

Stan chuckled, his blue eyes suddenly rueful. "Somehow I don't think Cameron will agree with you."

- 2 -

WITH SHAKING FINGERS Blair inserted her key into the brass lock of the old house she had once shared with Cameron, the grip she had kept on her emotions after Cameron's arrival at the party gradually slipping away. The gas lamps of Louisburg Square flickered in the midnight darkness, but for once she was in no mood to appreciate the charm of Beacon Hill. The chill wind that raced across the park to engulf her in an icy embrace touched her not at all.

Damn him! He had no right to do this to her. She had spent what seemed like an eternity putting him out of her life, out of her heart. The energy she had wasted on that man! Wasted. It was all wasted. He had only to appear before her, and it was like the last two years were only wisps of smoke—gone. The void she had filled with work was again a yawning chasm that threatened to swallow her. Only one person could fill the ache that now consumed her.

No! she screamed silently, terrified by her wayward thoughts. She had been down that road before, and it was a dead end, a lonely dead end. When the road got rough, when she really needed him, Cameron was nowhere to be found. He was always sidetracked, pulled off the beaten path by presidential elections, trouble in the Middle East, another war, another peace. Invariably she had been left to go on alone until he could catch up with her. But even then he never stayed for long.

Memories swept over her. The homecomings were so sweet, so joyous. Nothing mattered except that they were together again, free to love and cherish each other. But when the leave-takings began to intrude on the homecomings, it became a nightmare they couldn't escape by simply awakening.

She stiffened. No! She wouldn't let him reopen the door to the past. She slammed into the house, shutting out her tortured thoughts.

The firm footsteps that advanced to the foyer were only momentarily muffled by the resounding slam of the door. Margaret Johnson stood at the entrance to the living room, her matronly figure neatly encased in a black skirt and aqua blouse that beautifully complemented her white hair. She had been white-haired for as long as Blair could remember, but somehow she never looked old. Blair hoped she herself looked half as good when she was her mother's age.

"How was the party?"

Blair grimaced. "Don't ask." She hung up her coat and hastily changed the subject. "Thanks for baby-sitting, Mother. Did Julie give you any problem?"

"Not really. She didn't want to go back to sleep after Cameron left, but I convinced her she couldn't wait up for you. You know he's back in town, don't you?"

"Yes." Tension curled into her stomach. Cameron had made an immediate hit with her mother, and Margaret never missed the chance to let Blair know she thought the divorce was a mistake. Her urging for a reconciliation was one of the few things mother and daughter ever argued about, and Blair was in no mood for it tonight. She eyed Margaret warily. "He showed up at the party."

"I suspected he might." Margaret preceded her daughter

into the living room and took her favorite chair by the fire. When Blair settled into the wing chair across from her, she watched the green silk of Blair's dress float down about her and smiled. "Did he like your dress?"

"Who?" Blair asked, being deliberately obtuse. At her mother's reproving frown she sighed in exasperation. "Don't do this, Mother. I couldn't care less what Cameron thinks of my dress or anything else. I can hardly pretend he doesn't exist—he is, after all, Julie's father. But that's all he is to me."

"Baloney!" Margaret Johnson scoffed. "If you want to lie to yourself, go ahead. But you can't fool me. Look at yourself. You're nothing but skin and bones, and I haven't heard you laugh in months. You're miserable without Cameron; you're just too stubborn to admit it."

"I was miserable *with* him, in case you don't remember," Blair replied tiredly. She should have known from the beginning their marriage would never work. The eight-year difference in their ages had not been an insurmountable problem, but it was the experience he had gained in those years that had made him view Blair, at eighteen, as if she were merely a child. They were from two different worlds, with different values and goals. Nothing would ever change that.

But at eighteen, of course, she hadn't been able to see it. She was in love for the first time in her life, too caught up in the daydreams she was weaving to care about reality. It wasn't until later, when his ring was on her finger, that she realized Cameron didn't want the closeness she did. In fact, he didn't seem to want anything she wanted. He wanted to work, which he did with a vengeance. The long hours she was alone proved fertile ground for her growing resentment. Their marriage was doomed from the beginning.

Blair stared into the fire, stretching her hands out to the flames, frowning at the memories she saw dancing there. Dammit! She didn't want to talk about Cameron. All this talk was stirring up the ashes of a love she had fought to bury two years earlier. Why, after all this time, was everyone so fascinated with the subject of Cameron Wakefield?

She changed the subject. "Have you done most of your Christmas shopping?"

"Just about," her mother replied absently. "How about you?"

"I haven't made a dent in it," Blair admitted sheepishly. "This is the busiest time of the year for me. The girls are swamped with all the parties we're committed to arranging, not to mention the shopping for our clients. I've been helping them out with the shopping and trying to keep on top of everything in the office, so I haven't had much time for anything else."

"I suppose Cameron will buy the toy stores out before he goes back to London. Did he say when he was leaving?"

"No." Blair leaned back in her chair, desperately wanting to avoid telling her mother the truth, but knowing that was impossible. She might as well get it over with. "Actually," she admitted slowly, "Cameron's not going back to London. He bought the *Gazette*."

"He what?" Margaret Johnson exclaimed, stunned. "Why would he do such a thing? Everyone knows it's about to fold. No one reads the *Gazette!*"

"Yes, I know," Blair responded wearily, "but Cameron has visions of changing that."

"He'll do all right," her mother replied confidently. "After all, he's got plenty of incentive. With Julie needing a full-time father and you needing a husband, he has to succeed."

"I don't need a husband," Blair countered irritably.

"That's a matter of opinion," Margaret Johnson said knowingly. "You and Cameron made some mistakes in your marriage, but your feelings for him are the same as they were the day you first met. You love him, honey, and the divorce hasn't changed that."

Scenes of that meeting came to mind and pushed all other thoughts aside. Blair had gone to a Saint Patrick's Day party with a girl friend from high school, convinced to attend only when Michelle refused to go alone. Blair was even less enthusiastic when she saw the crowd of people packed into the tiny apartment. Most of the guests were in some way connected with the *Tribune*, but to Blair they were a roomful of rowdy strangers. Somehow she and Michelle got separated; the lights were turned low, and suddenly the press of bodies was too much. She bolted for the door and collided hard with a warm, male body.

"Whoa, sweetheart. What's the rush?"

She had looked up into the blackest eyes she had ever seen, surrounded by long, thick lashes she would have loved to claim for herself. Warm with laughter and something else she was too inexperienced to recognize, his gaze traveled the contours of her face, and the hands that had reached out to steady her were suddenly drawing her closer. "You can't leave yet. We haven't danced."

She had every intention of telling him no, of pulling herself free and making a quick escape. But when his arms went around her, her protests died in her throat. He led her in a slow, sensual rhythm that tripled the pounding of her heart and robbed her of her will. She was mesmerized. Being in his arms was the most natural thing in the world. She didn't even know his name, but it didn't matter. There was an instant attraction between them that couldn't be denied.

That was the beginning. Cameron had kept her by his side all evening, and when he finally took her home, his kiss claimed her heart and soul, calling up a passion she hadn't known existed. It was such a beautiful beginning. But like all good things, it had come to an end. And that she couldn't, wouldn't, think about. "I don't want to discuss Cameron. Or his paper. So let's drop it, okay? It's been a long day and I'm tired."

That was the wrong thing to say. Margaret Johnson's face set in firm lines of disapproval. "Of course you're tired. You're running yourself ragged with this ridiculous business of yours. I didn't like the idea when you first came up with it, and I still don't like it. Surrogate wife to a bunch of bachelors." She sniffed in disdain. "If you want a husband, marry Cameron again, for godsake! But don't go from one man's apartment to another!"

Tired as she was, Blair couldn't summon the angry defense her mother obviously expected. She laughed. "Mother, Maid-In-Heaven is a legitimate business, as you well know...."

Her mother sighed audibly as Blair tried and failed to suppress the grin that tugged the corner of her mouth. Her mother was always so proper, so exceedingly correct. Just once she wished Margaret would appreciate the outrageous. "I guess I should warn you about tomorrow. There's going to be a writeup about Maid-In-Heaven in the morning paper. Stan set it up. It's going to be great publicity."

"Is that really necessary?"

"Well, of course it is. It's free advertising." Determination pushed away the laughter that lingered in her eyes. "You're worrying for nothing, Mother. The feedback I've gotten has been overwhelmingly positive. You have no reason to be morally outraged. Sex is *not* one of the services I offer. My clients can get that elsewhere."

"Blair!"

"Well, it's true."

"I don't want to discuss it. I must get home. Your father will be wondering where I am." She retrieved the needlepoint she had been working on and headed for the entrance hall, where she hurriedly pulled on her coat.

"Why didn't Daddy come with you tonight?" Blair asked. "I know he doesn't like it when you're out this late by yourself."

The older woman looked up the stairs conspiratorially and whispered, "He's making Julie a dollhouse for Christmas. You should see it. It even has lights."

"Oh, Mother, she'll love it!" She reached over to give Margaret a swift hug. "Thanks again for baby-sitting. And don't worry about me; everything is fine."

After her mother left, Blair slipped the safety chain into place and pictured her father pacing the floor with one eye on the clock and the other on the door. Her parents were more in love at that moment than they had been the day they married. Problems had buffeted them over the years, but their love remained constant, creating a force field that left them untouched by outside influences. That was what

Made in Heaven 27

Blair herself had wanted with Cameron and what she had missed.

She snapped off the living-room lights. In the darkness, which was eased only by the lamps in the square, her shoulders drooped, weighted by a fatigue that was enervating. That's all it is... fatigue, she told herself firmly as she trudged upstairs. After what she'd been through that night, she had a right to feel drained. A good night's sleep would dispel the exhaustion and inexplicable loneliness that had suddenly swamped her.

In her own room Blair kicked off her high-heeled sandals, which had been pinching her feet for hours. A chill slid down her spine when she stripped off her party finery, and the baby-blue flannel nightgown she pulled on offered a comforting warmth. If her mother could see her now, her fears would be laid to rest. Women who conducted clandestine affairs didn't sleep in flannel nightgowns!

Chuckling softly, she jumped into bed and choked on her laughter when her bare legs touched the sheets. God, it was cold! No one should have to sleep alone on a night like this. If Cameron were there...

The shrill buzz of the doorbell suddenly shattered the quiet of the house. Blair stiffened, certainty sinking to the pit of her stomach with a sickening thud. Cameron. It had to be. Who else would have the audacity to turn up on her doorstep at one o'clock in the morning? She knew that their discussion was by no means finished, that he would show up sooner or later. But that night? She wasn't ready for it. She needed more time.

Had she conjured him up with her thoughts? Damn her thoughts! She had spent two years forgetting him. His return to Boston didn't change that. He wasn't going to walk back into her life and her bed as though nothing had happened!

Resolutely she rolled onto her side and pulled the quilt up over her shoulder. The buzzing of the bell turned into short, impatient staccato rings, but she ignored the clamor. He could stand out in the cold all night for all she cared. He'd soon grow tired of his childish game and go away. She wasn't going to answer the door.

Five minutes later Cameron leaned on the bell for a full minute, and Blair's resolve withered under a blaze of anger. The bell was screaming like a banshee, loud enough to wake the dead—which was just what he'd be if he didn't stop.

She jerked on her robe and ran downstairs, twin flags of color riding high in her cheeks. Without bothering to release the safety chain, she yanked open the door as far as it would go and gasped as a frigid blast of air slapped her in the face. Her toes curled under on the bare floor, and she wrapped her arms around her shivering body and glared at the man on her doorstep. He looked like the Devil himself standing there, his dark hair and topcoat blending in with the blackness of the night, casting him in shadows. From a face that was all angles and planes, his grin flashed sparkling white, echoing the teasing laughter in his eyes.

Blair could feel her anger evaporating under the sudden rush of desire that took her by surprise, horrifying her. Furiously she reminded herself that the icy wind playing with his hair was also slipping under her gown to run up her bare legs, and he had the gall to stand there grinning like it was the middle of summer. "What do you want?"

"You said we could talk at your office. I understand your office is here, at home. Well, here I am." Lazily he straightened from his slump against the doorbell, his craggy brow quirking in amusement at her defensive stance as his eyes made a languorous sweep of her and missed nothing. "Are you going to let me in or not?"

"Not on your life!" she choked. "I told you at the party we had nothing to say to each other." How dare he think he had only to smile that crooked grin and she would greet him with open arms! He couldn't come in. She hadn't missed his masculine appraisal of her. It was just a little too knowing and a lot too dangerous, vividly reminding her of her nakedness under her gown. What was it he had said at the party? He was tired of sleeping alone? Well, so was she, but to let him get any closer would be sheer madness. Her heart was already pounding double time. "Go away, Cameron. My office hours are eight-thirty to five. Come back then."

"Do you want the whole neighborhood to hear our little discussion?" A thread of steel ran through his softly spoken words. "Don't push me, Blair. I want to talk to you, and I'm not leaving until I do. Whether we talk in private or in front of all the neighbors is entirely up to you."

She wavered, torn between wisely giving in to his demands and slamming the door in his face. He probably wouldn't hesitate to awaken the neighborhood. She knew from past experience that he was the most stubborn man she had ever met. When he wanted his way, he usually got it. His tenaciousness was one of the first things that had attracted her to him. Marriage to him had taught her to be stubborn, too. But she wasn't stupid.

Carefully she released the safety chain. "Come in, but keep your voice down."

"Don't worry, I'm not going to wake Julie." As if he had every right in the world, he walked unerringly into the living room of the house they had once shared, switched on a lamp by the couch, and headed for the small bar in the corner. After pouring himself a drink, he dropped onto the couch, his feet extended before him on the coffee table.

She ground her teeth in frustration. "Don't make yourself too comfortable. You're not staying."

"Don't be too sure of that."

"I'm not going to argue with you, Cameron. You made your opinion of me quite clear at the party."

"What did I say?" he demanded, his dark brows lifted in an attempt at innocence that didn't fool her for a minute. "I haven't seen you in two years. You're the mother of my daughter. Is it so unnatural for me to be interested in what you've been doing?"

"Yes. Dammit, Cameron, we're divorced!"

"A mere technicality," he replied, waving aside her objections with a lazy grin. "Why don't you tell me what your real relationship with Stan is."

"No, I don't think so," she said lightly over the pounding of her heart. When he smiled at her like that, her knees turned to water and she had to remind herself that her private life was none of his business.

She sank into the chair across from him, watching him warily. He had changed. Oh, he still had the dark good looks he had always had—the chiseled cheekbones and square chin that could be uncompromising yet ruggedly attractive at one and the same time. Now and then she caught a flash of the boyishness that had been so endearing, but the mischievous twinkle in his eyes had a tendency to harden into a glint of determination that would brook no refusals. Two years' time had added a touch of gray to his temples and furrows at the corner of his eyes. He was still the handsomest man she had ever seen, but he was not the same one who had once chased her up a tree into his boyhood treehouse, where they had spent the afternoon making love. He was more mature, more wary, than she remembered.

"Why did you move back to Boston?" she asked abruptly, eyeing him curiously.

"Julie's here. You're here."

His soft words touched her like a caress and evoked feelings she had to close her eyes to. Don't let him do this to me, she thought frantically. She knew how he operated; she'd been a victim of his charm too many times not to know what he was up to. The intense concentration on her, the mesmerizing effect of his eyes—it was all designed to make a woman feel as if there were nothing that mattered to him quite as much as she. This was a heady feeling. While it lasted. "Stan told me you bought the *Gazette*," she said desperately, grasping at conversational straws. "He thinks—"

A dark brow lifted wryly. "I can just imagine what he thinks. That I'm going to steal his business? He's right. But it won't hurt him. Boston needs two papers. Maybe now the *Tribune* reporters will get up off their lazy butts and dig up some real stories instead of just relying on the wire services."

"But why?" she persisted. "Two years ago you couldn't leave fast enough." She swallowed the bitter accusations that trembled on her tongue. "Didn't the job of foreign correspondent turn out the way you expected?"

"Not particularly. You know that old saying: 'Be careful what you wish for; you just may get it.'" He leaned forward to set his glass on the coffee table, and his eyes captured hers. "Tell me about Maid-In-Heaven," he commanded softly.

Blair bristled. "What do you want to know?"

"Everything." He laughed at the suspicion clearly revealed in her eyes. "Come on, Blair, I'm not asking for your company's financial statement. Just give me a few details. I really am interested."

"Why? So you can make snide remarks like you did at the party?" she demanded.

His jaw clenched in an obvious effort to control his impatience. "I'm sorry about anything I might have said then. I'm sure it was totally out of line. Chalk it up to the fact that it was the first time I had seen my wife with another man."

"I am not your wife!" she reminded him hotly. "And that was no excuse for your rudeness to Stan. Maid-In-Heaven wouldn't be what it is today if it hadn't been for him. He's the one who gave me the idea—"

"Good old Stan," he cut in mockingly.

"That's right," she exclaimed angrily. "He was always there when I needed him. He knew that this type of work would give me a chance to be with Julie. It also put food on the table and paid the bills."

"If you needed more money for Julie's support, you could have written," Cameron said quietly, reproachfully.

And what about my support? her heart cried. Didn't he realize that his money was a cold comfort? She had needed him, and work offered the only balm that could soothe her wounded heart. "No, Cameron, I couldn't." Pride, if nothing else, had held her back, though she'd thought of contacting him innumerable times.

"No, I guess not."

She drew in a shuddering breath and flashed a smile that was a mockery of her real smile. "Anyway, I took on Stan as a client, and the business seemed to mushroom. Caroline

Vickers helped me out during the first six months, but we couldn't handle all the work, so I eventually had to hire three more women."

"And how did you come up with the name? Did Stan think of that, too?"

She shot him an impatient glare. "No. I came up with it one day when I was explaining the company's services to a prospective client. We're really offering our clients the best of two worlds. They get a 'wife' who doesn't nag or move her mother in. And my employees have the satisfaction of taking care of several 'husbands' without having to give up their personal lives. For both parties it really is a marriage made in heaven."

"Which is more than can be said for ours," he mumbled, half under his breath.

His self-deprecating words took her by surprise. Was that regret she heard in his voice? "Cameron..."

"So," he interrupted, shaking off his sudden gloom to give her a teasing grin, "you're a successful businesswoman. I'm impressed." He got to his feet in one swift, lithe movement and headed for the bar to refill his drink. When he lifted his glass in silent inquiry, she shook her head. "Somehow I didn't think a career was what you were after. I thought Prince Charming and a vine-covered cottage would hold more appeal for you. You didn't meet anyone?" He eyed her surreptitiously from beneath half-closed lids; for the first time he seemed almost vulnerable.

"I didn't say that," she denied, unable to suppress a smile at this not-too-subtle line of questioning. He was dying to know what she'd been doing for the last two years. "I've been out a few times, here and there, but Julie and work didn't leave much time for a social life."

"Thank God!" he exclaimed, dimples flashing as he grinned broadly. "I know I made a lousy Prince Charming, but at least you haven't found someone else to fill the role."

How could she? she thought wildly. No one else had even raised her blood pressure, but her pride would never let her admit that. "All right, Cameron. Enough of this nonsense. What do you want?'

"You."

She choked, her widened eyes caught in the trap of his. So he was serious.

"No!" she cried hoarsely. She wouldn't open her heart to him again. She couldn't survive such pain, such soul-destroying agony, a second time. She jumped to her feet. "We've had our talk. Now you should leave."

"Not just yet," he replied tightly. His onyx eyes darkened, their bottomless depths lighted by what could only be sparks of pure determination. "I'm not leaving until we finish this discussion. And we haven't yet."

Hysterical laughter rippled from her, and in a voice that was not quite steady she demanded, "What is there to discuss? You had your life planned long before you met me. A career in the newspaper business was all you wanted. To hell with your father's plans for you to join his company. You were going to make it on your own as a reporter—climb your way to the top and eventually own your own paper. Well, congratulations. You made it."

She bit her lip and prayed that the hurt she had experienced at this man's hands wasn't reflected in her eyes. "There was only one thing wrong with your plan. You made no allowances for me, your wife. I was an afterthought, something you tried to squeeze in at the last minute. You knew it wouldn't work two years ago. Why should it work now? What has changed?"

"You. Me. Our lives." He set his untouched drink on the bar and advanced toward her, his eyes, his voice, his body, entreating her to listen. "We made some mistakes, Blair, but do we have to pay for them the rest of our lives?" When she stubbornly refused to answer, he pulled her up in front of him and gave her a gentle shake. "You've changed in the last two years, really grown up...."

With a strangled cry she tore herself free of his grasp, her emerald eyes wide and wary, frightened. She wouldn't let him do this. God, she knew how persuasive he could be. Why was she standing there listening, giving him the chance to break down the defenses she had built with tears spilled over him? She lashed out at him. "You always did blame our problems on my age. 'Poor Blair, she's such an innocent. She's got her head in the clouds and her heart in a fairy tale.'"

"That's right. You wanted too much out of marriage—more than a man can give."

"I wanted *you*," she cried, "not a part-time husband who only came home for a change of clothes and a shave."

"Those days are gone, Blair. I own the paper now. There won't be any more separations." In one stride he eliminated the distance between them. His velvety voice was soft and oh, so convincing. "The divorce was a mistake, sweetheart. Admit it. You've been just as miserable without me as I've been without you. I'm sure of it. We can make it work again. Just give us a chance."

The clean, spicy fragrance that she would always associate with him surrounded her, enfolding her in bittersweet memories. It took every ounce of willpower she possessed to harden her heart against him, but she did it. She had to. She couldn't let him hurt her again.

"You're forgetting that it didn't work the first time," she reminded him coolly. "And nothing has really changed. Yes, I'm two years older and wiser. I've matured. But I still want the same things I've always wanted. You can't be the husband I want and need."

"Why not?" he demanded, frowning.

"Because you love your work more than anything else on this earth. I won't take second billing in your life, Cameron. That may be selfish of me, but it's how I am." Her eyes met his unflinchingly. "You told me one time how you resented the fact that your father never had time for you when you were growing up. He never took you fishing or even played a game of basketball with you. And your mother always made excuses for him. I won't do that with Julie."

"You won't have to. Believe me, honey, I'll be there for both of you."

She shook her head stubbornly. "No, Cameron. It's over."

He cocked a mocking eyebrow at her, a devilish grin taunting her. "You really think so?" Slowly, insidiously, his arms wrapped around her to pull her toward him, easily overcoming her resistance until her breasts touched his chest. When she stiffened, his soft laughter feathered her ear. "Do you honestly think a few words spoken by a judge can end what's between us?"

He reached up to trace the curve of her brow, her cheek, her mouth. His fingers were tender and all too knowing, rubbing against her lips like a cat licking cream. He slipped his fingers into her mouth to run it over the edge of her teeth, and Blair thought she would die. When she couldn't stand the sensual assault another minute, he lifted her chin and forced her to look at him. "Does that feel like it's over between us?" he asked huskily.

She quivered in his grasp, racked by a maelstrom of conflicting emotions. Doors she had barred two years ago strained against their locks and broke free, their release echoing in the most private chambers of her heart. Her desires flowed through a soul that had been empty for too long. Desperately, futilely, she tried to dam them with words. "There's no place in my life for you now. I have all the husbands I need."

"Those don't count." He could sense her weakening; she could see it in his eyes. "I'm going to court you all over again. We'll start out fresh, and this time we won't mess things up. We will work it out, sweetheart. I never stopped wanting you. You gave yourself to me when you were eighteen. And what's mine I keep."

He bent his head toward her, his gaze fastened on her mouth. Panic coursed through her. "No, Cameron! Don't! I don't want you to..."

"Are you sure?" he murmured huskily, his breath mingling with hers. "Kiss you? Touch you? Make love to you till dawn?" His hand began a slow, seductive climb, moving up her arm to her shoulder before coming to rest on her neck, his thumb teasing the pulse that fluttered there. "What do you want, sweetheart? Tell me."

She stared at him, unable to break the invisible bond that stretched between them. A sweet tide of half-forgotten longing swept over her, and she knew he felt it, too. She saw it reflected in the burning depths of his eyes, felt it in the tightening of his body. The past intruded on the present, and time slipped away. The look in his eyes was so achingly familiar, calling to the deep core of passion that only he could touch. Suddenly nothing was as important as touching him, kissing him. Without conscious thought she melted against him.

"Are you sure you don't want me?" he growled, triumph lighting his eyes. He molded her to his hard frame, the exploring fingers of one hand slipping inside the collar of her nightgown to caress the throbbing firmness of her breasts.

Her body welcomed his touch, gloried in it. She closed her eyes against the intense pleasure his fingers evoked and was shocked at the low moan that erupted from her throat. God, she had missed him!

"We never had any problems in bed, did we?"

No, they never had. One kiss and she melted; one husky murmur and the world receded, pushed aside by a need so strong that it threatened to consume them both. It was happening all over again, and she couldn't seem to stop it. She knew she would regret it the next day. It would change nothing, least of all the loneliness and heartache of the past two years, but she desperately needed to feel him, taste him.

A crooked grin tugged at the corner of his mouth, but his eyes lost all traces of amusement. Slowly, as if savoring the very essence of her soft skin, he planted hot, searing kisses on her throat and shoulders, starting a fire in her at the very core of her being. When he nipped at her ear, a shudder of longing shook her, and she knew he couldn't help but be aware of his effect on her. Instantly his hold on her tightened before he deliberately pushed her away from him.

Blair stared at him in disbelief, her heart racing with frustrated desire, and he only smiled ruefully. "It hurts, doesn't it? And it's going to hurt a lot more before it gets better." Almost tenderly he smoothed back the curling wisps of sandy hair at her temples. "Don't misunderstand me, sweetheart. I want you, and I certainly mean to have you. But this time we're going to take it slow. This is too important to rush. When you ache for me, when you've endured the endless nights I have, you'll see that nothing and no one is as important as the two of us being together. *Then* I'll do something about it." He leaned over and gave her a swift, hard kiss that was infinitely frustrating in its brevity. "Sweet dreams, love."

- 3 -

"I'M MOVING INTO the house next week, Mrs. Wakefield, and I've got to have some help. I know nothing about decorating or arranging a kitchen. I was hoping you could find someone to help me. I haven't got a lot of time that I can devote to this, and I'd like to have everything done before Christmas. When I read the article about Maid-In-Heaven in the paper, I realized you were just what I've needed...."

The man droned on and on. Blair nodded and smiled in what she hoped was an understanding way and thankfully didn't hear a word he said. Absently she tapped a pencil against the edge of the desk she had installed in what used to be the downstairs guest room but which was now her "office." The dull sound of the impatient jabs was a fitting accompaniment for the restless swinging of her booted foot. She was the picture of professionalism, her scarlet tie blouse a bright splash of color against the charcoal gray of her suit, but beneath the cool facade, anxiety ran rampant, taunting her relentlessly, twisting her nerves. The demanding business she faced daily when she entered this part of her house receded to the edges of her consciousness, and she saw instead the empty days, endured again the sleepless agony of the past six nights.

How subtle was Cameron's form of torture. He was back in her life, yet he wasn't, disrupting her routine, her heart, without half trying. She hadn't seen him since the night of the party; her only contact with him had been his nightly phone calls to Julie. And every night Julie never failed to give her a report on those calls. "Daddy's going to buy me a new dress. And cowboy boots! Daddy had cowboy boots when he was little like me."

Blair closed her eyes weakly against the remembered chattering of her daughter, picturing her in cowboy boots and wondering what Cameron had been like at age four. Did Julie get her impatience from him? She never walked when she could run, her long wavy chestnut hair flying like a banner behind her. And no secret was too insignificant for her to investigate. She was a miniature feminine version of her father, her brown eyes not as dark as his but just as perceptive, her easy grin and teasing dimples a sure sign of the mischievousness that was never far below the surface. She had inherited her high cheekbones and pert nose from Blair, but her stubborn chin was a chip off of Cameron's.

Julie had been without a father for too long, and Cameron was quickly making up for the years he had missed. She had squealed in delight when he had a bouquet of balloons delivered to her; she had been thoroughly enchanted with the gift. Cameron's special attention had added an extra sparkle to her brown eyes and a brightness to her smile. Blair's heart melted as she recalled the excitement dancing over her daughter's elfin features when she came running in from nursery school, her impatience as she waited for Cameron's nightly calls. Julie was thrilled with his return to her life, and reluctantly Blair had to admit that Cameron was once again a force to contend with.

But his absence made Blair's nights pure hell. She was too restless to sleep, her slumber haunted by a dark-haired giant of a man who seduced her with his words and mouth before slipping into the nebulous clouds of her dreams, leaving her with an ache she couldn't assuage. She couldn't close her eyes without seeing him, feeling him. In desperation she tossed and turned, frantically trying to escape the heightened senses he had so effortlessly aroused, but to no avail. His ghost was there, in her bedroom, in her bed, and she couldn't escape.

"I hope this isn't going to cause you a problem, Mrs. Wakefield. I know I've given you very little notice, but it can't be helped. You really should advertise more. Here is the new address, and if you'll just have someone there when the movers arrive..."

Blair jerked back to attention, cursing herself for allowing her mind to wander during a business discussion. "I am sorry, Mr. Kelly," she interrupted him firmly, "but I'm afraid I can't help you. All of my employees are booked through the holidays, so I won't be accepting any new clients until January."

"But I need help now!"

"Have you tried a professional decorator? Or the moving company?" she suggested.

"Yes, but neither of them provide that type of service."

"The only way I can help you is if you postpone the move for several weeks. I'm in the process of hiring several more employees, and someone will be available by then to assist you." She rose to her feet, effectively ending their discussion. "I'm sorry I can't be of more help, but if you decide to postpone the move, call me in a few weeks and we'll set up a work schedule."

Blair sighed when her office door closed behind the man's retreating back. She collapsed into her chair. What ever possessed her to let Stan run that article about her? She'd been inundated with prospective clients, men and women too caught up in their professional careers to look after their private lives. They all wanted her services, and they wanted them right away. She felt like she was being pulled in a hundred different directions and going nowhere. And every time the phone rang, every time someone knocked at the door, she caught herself listening for a certain voice, looking for a familiar thatch of dark hair. Damn him! It had been a week. What had happened to his plans to court her until she was aching for him? The only ache she felt at that moment was pure, unadulterated rage.

"If looks could kill, I'd be in big trouble right now," Caroline Vickers said from the doorway, her brown eyes twinkling with the outrageous sense of humor that rarely deserted her. Caroline's office had been carved out of what used to be the study. "What did Old Man Kelly say to you, for godsakes?"

Blair laughed in spite of the tension that still held her in its grip. "He didn't say anything. And he's not old, Caroline. He's only thirty-five."

"I've seen his type before. He's thirty-five going on a hundred." She sank into the chair in front of Blair's desk and grinned broadly. "He probably sleeps in a nightshirt, calls his mother every night, and wears his rubbers when it rains. I bet he's looking for a little woman to warm his slippers by the fire and bring him the paper. Doesn't he know he can train a dog to do that? Of course," she continued candidly, "a dog can't say 'Yes, dear, anything you say, dear.'"

Blair chuckled. "How does Mike put up with you?" If ever there was anyone less likely to adopt a meek, subservient role, it was Caroline Vickers. Five feet ten in her stocking feet, she was a magnificent woman of Junoesque proportions and not adverse to throwing her weight around should the occasion warrant it. Underneath her sometimes blunt exterior, however, beat the heart of a pussycat. With her husband's amused indulgence she collected strays— kids, dogs, bachelors. As part-time secretary/office manager and occasional 'wife' to a handful of bachelors, she was Blair's right hand, and best friend.

"Not all our clients can be Mr. Right, Caroline. That's one of the hazards of our trade."

"I'd settle for fifty-fifty," she grumbled.

"And what would Mike say to that?" Blair teased.

"Oh, he trusts me," Caroline replied airily. "If he didn't, he wouldn't dare let me around all these bachelors."

Made in Heaven

Envy shot through Blair, catching at her heart and adjusting her vision to the sunless depths of the ocean. Caroline and Mike were soul mates, each the completing half of the other. Together they were whole, apart and separate from the rest of the world, a fact that was obvious any time they were together. After sixteen years of marriage they still held hands, still gravitated toward each other in a crowd. Did they have any idea how lucky they were?

"Do you want to tell me what's been troubling you?" Caroline asked quietly, her round face furrowed with worry.

"I'm just tired." Tired of fighting the truth that had dodged her footsteps ever since the night of Stan's party. Regardless of how painful it was, she had to face facts. Cameron had never said that he loved her, only that he wanted her. They were good in bed together. Face it, Blair, a hurt voice cried from her heart, the two of you were terrific together, in bed. That's what he misses. Nothing more, nothing less.

"Are you sure that's all it is?"

"Of course. You know this place has been a madhouse this week. If you weren't helping me with the business and Anna wasn't watching over Julie after she gets out of nursery school, I'd probably be climbing the walls right now."

The older woman beamed proudly. "Anna's a good kid, if I do say so myself. And she loves baby-sitting Julie. She's going to make a great mother one of these days." The maternal light in her brown eyes sharpened. "Don't change the subject. Have you looked in the mirror lately? You look like death warmed over."

"Thanks," Blair said wryly. When Caroline's mood didn't lighten she warned, "Don't try that mother hen act on me. I'm not one of your chicks."

"Someone obviously needs to watch over you. You're doing a lousy job all by yourself," she retorted bluntly. "Is it Julie? Do you still think enrolling her in nursery school was a mistake? I know you want to spend as much time as possible with her, but—"

"No, it's not that. She needs to be with other kids. She's been around adults for too long. Anyway, she loves it. I . . ." The ringing of the bell attached to the front door cut her off, and she sighed in relief. "You go take care of whoever that is while I look over these applications. I've got to hire someone soon."

"All right. I'll let you off the hook... this time. But one day soon we're going to have a long talk."

But not today, Blair thought as Caroline shut the office door behind her. Right now her emotions were too volatile to discuss with anyone, even Caroline. Over the last few years it had been Caroline's wisecracking, almost irreverent remarks that had helped her over the rough spots after the divorce. But what could she say now other than the obvious? Within hours of his return to Boston, Cameron had cracked the protective armor it had taken her two years to build. Lord, she should have never let him in the house!

"Blair..." Caroline stood in the doorway again, her face wreathed in confusion. She glanced over her shoulder, then back to Blair. "Cameron is here to see you."

He was there at last. Electrical sparks of excitement shot through her, but they were ruthlessly doused with cold self-contempt. What an idiot she was! For the better part of a week he had practically ignored her; yet, when he finally did put in an appearance, she was ready to throw herself on his chest like a love-starved widow. "Tell him I'm out," she said flatly. "Tell him anything you like. Just don't let him in here."

"Are you trying to avoid me?" Cameron drawled softly from the doorway, running his eyes over her as if hungry for the very sight of her.

Blair's heart lurched in her breast. Despite the very proper gray flannel suit he wore, there was a rakish, devil-may-care grin on his face that did strange things to her pulse rate. No man had a right to look so sexy, she thought in irritation. "I'm not avoiding you. I'm busy."

"I only want a few minutes." He strode purposefully into the room and flashed Caroline a smile. "How's Mike? And how are the kids?"

"Fine. We're all fine." She glanced from Cameron's smiling face to Blair's taut one. "How long have you been in town?" she asked suspiciously.

"A week. Didn't Blair tell you?"

"No, but I should have guessed."

Blair groaned. She could see the wheels clicking in Caroline's head, with all the pieces falling neatly into place to explain her moodiness of late, the strange restlessness that had distracted her at the oddest times. It irritated her terribly that Caroline should assume Cameron was at the root of her problems. She glared at the problem in question and snapped, "There was no reason to tell Caroline you were back. It wasn't important." If he didn't get that message, he was dense!

Cameron grinned, his dark eyes laughing at her indulgently. "I can see my work's cut out for me." He turned to Caroline, who was watching them in fascination. "I'm trying to convince Blair to give me a second chance, Caroline. But so far she's resisting the idea."

"Soliciting Caroline's help won't do you any good," Blair warned him. "I have no intention of changing my mind, so you may as well accept it. The answer is still no."

Cameron's dark brow quirked, the dimples in each cheek threatening to deepen in amusement. "You know I won't give up so easily, Blair." He turned to Caroline, placing his arm around her broad shoulders to steer her toward the door. "As you can see, Caroline, she's going to be stubborn. We've got a few things to discuss. Will you guard the door while I try to talk some sense into this woman?"

"Of course," Caroline replied promptly.

"Don't you dare play along with him, Caroline," Blair called out in sudden panic. "I want him thrown out of here right this minute!"

Caroline only grinned and shut the door smartly behind her. Cameron laughed and turned to face her, his eyes dancing. "Too late, Blair. Looks like you're stuck with me for a while."

She refused to meet his eyes. She reached for the applications she had spent all afternoon trying to wade through, but hastily dropped them when she saw how badly her fingers were shaking. "You're wasting your time, Cameron. I don't know why you suddenly decided to put in an appearance, but it won't do you any good. I can't be bothered with you this afternoon. I have too much work to do."

He took one of the two chairs that flanked her desk, his long legs stretched out in front of him, the gray flannel pulled across his muscular thighs. The lightheartedness he'd shown in front of Caroline vanished, and in its stead was a guardedness that tightened the chiseled lines of his face. Searchingly his eyes ran over her stiff figure before he finally asked quietly, "Did Julie like the balloons?"

"You know she did," Blair replied, unbending a little as she remembered her daughter's excitement. "She insisted on sleeping with some of them, but they kept pulling the blankets off her."

Cameron chuckled. "I wish I could have seen that. Maybe next time . . ." He looked at her expectantly, but when she stubbornly refused to offer any encouragement, irritation wrinkled his brow. "Are you ticked off because I didn't send you any balloons?"

"Of course not!" Did he actually think she was jealous of her own daughter? She could have kissed him for his display of love toward Julie. No, it was his continued presence in her dreams that she resented. "But from now on I think we should discuss any plans you make for her *before* you tell her."

Enlightenment dawned on Cameron, amusement brightening his eyes. "You're sore because I haven't talked to you all week. I am sorry, sweetheart, but this has been an unusually busy time, and I really didn't think you wanted to talk to me anyway." He spread his arms and grinned at her guilelessly. "Well, here I am. What's on your mind?"

You, her heart groaned, but she said stiffly, "I want you to be careful with Julie. She was spared the trauma of our divorce by being so young. Don't start something you don't intend to continue."

"I'm not," he replied, his eyes reproaching her. "Believe me, I'd never do anything to hurt either one of you."

"Then don't tell her any of this nonsense about us getting back together. She'd only get her hopes up for nothing. You've been in town a week and where have you spent your time? At the paper. I think that says it all, don't you?"

"No, I don't. The *Gazette*'s in trouble now. It's going to take a lot of work to get it back on its feet. But it won't always be that way. There will be time for us." At her skeptical look he sighed, "I meant every word I said after Stan's party. I won't give up."

He perched on the edge of her desk, his hip resting dangerously close to her arm. Before she could move back, he grabbed her hand and trapped it against his thigh, easily holding it captive there despite its fluttering attempts to escape. His eyes burned into hers. "Have dinner with me tonight," he commanded softly.

"I can't."

"Why not?" he demanded. "Do you have another date?"

"No, I have to work."

"Then we'll make it tomorrow night."

"Sorry, I'm all booked up."

"Monday night?" he asked. Blair shook her head, and the frown that had been hovering in the depths of his eyes descended on his brow in full force. "Quit giving me the runaround. You have to eat. And what about Julie? If you're working, who's going to watch her?"

"She's going with me." She bit back the laughter that suddenly convulsed her, knowing Cameron could see it in her eyes. Talk about poetic justice. For years he had never found time for her, and now that the shoe was on the other foot, he didn't like it at all.

"And just what type of work are you doing that you can take Julie along?"

"We're going shopping." At his surprised look she laughed out loud. "It's one of the services I provide for my clients. Most bachelors are notoriously bad shoppers, so I take that worry off their hands. They just tell me how much they want to spend and a little bit about the person who's receiving the gift, and I take it from there. Of course, I don't usually do this personally. All my employees are excellent shoppers, but they're swamped with so much other work right now that I'm helping out."

"And I suppose you're going to be busy with this right

up until Christmas Eve?" he ventured, his thumb absently running across the back of her hand in a gentle caress.

"Well, yes," she admitted weakly, distracted by the feel of his skin against hers. It was an innocent gesture, the holding of hands, but she'd never realized just how devastating it could be. Her nerve endings sprang to life at the lightest movement of his fingers, short-circuiting her breathing and forcing blood through her veins until she was lightheaded. Did he have any idea what he was doing to her? In growing panic she tried to tug her hand free, but his hold only tightened. Desperately she tried to bring her mind back to their conversation. "As soon as I've finished shopping for clients, I have to buy some things for Julie. Would you like to stay with her for a couple of evenings next week?"

"Yes, of course." He studied her thoughtfully. "You're not going to make this easy for me, are you?"

"What?" she asked in confusion.

"Courting you," he explained softly. He tossed her hand back in her lap and stood up to pace restlessly before her. Blair watched in fascination as frustration darkened his eyes and lowered his brows to a fierce frown. He looked like a little boy who had been denied an extra cookie and couldn't understand why. "How the hell am I supposed to court you if you won't spend any time with me?" he asked indignantly. "Can't you put the past behind us and start fresh?"

How could she when the past was so much a part of the present? she wondered in bewilderment. She couldn't walk through the house without tripping over a memory. She couldn't deny the years they had together, the love, the pain. She didn't want to start over. They had to continue, hopefully wiser than they were before.

"I'm not trying to put up roadblocks," she finally said quietly. "But you can't expect me to drop everything I've worked so hard for in the last two years just because you've decided to come back into my life. Maid-In-Heaven is very important to me, just as your paper is to you. I have responsibilities, and I'm not going to neglect them."

"We seem to be at an impasse. Any suggestions?"

Blair shook her head mutely. She almost wished he would

Made in Heaven

sweep her into his arms and carry her up the stairs to the room they had once shared, saving her the pain of making a decision. It would be so easy to reach out and touch him, to take what they both wanted and damn the consequences. Only self-preservation kept her hands at her side. She couldn't encourage her own destruction, but neither could she turn her back on the temptation he presented.

"If you can't beat 'em, join 'em," he said resignedly. "If you only have time for your clients, I'll just have to become a client."

Blair jumped as if she'd been stung. "Don't be ridiculous!"

"I'm not," he replied. "It's really the only logical solution. With both of us so tied up in our own careers, the only way we'll have time to see each other is if one of us becomes involved in the other's career. I need someone to take care of my apartment, and if I'm going to rent a wife, you're the one I want to rent."

"Oh, no you don't," she said flatly. "I'm not the prize in this ridiculous game you're playing. I no longer work directly with the clients. I don't have time." When he started to interrupt, she gestured impatiently at their surroundings. "Look at this place. I'm snowed under now just trying to keep up with my employees and clients, not to mention all the paperwork. I can't walk away from all this to spend time with you."

"What about Stan? If you weren't working directly with him, I don't know what you'd call it."

"But that was only for a special occasion. And Stan's a friend."

"And what am I?" Cameron growled. "The enemy?"

"No, but—"

"No *but*'s. I know you can spare three evenings a week for me. For *us*. Unless, of course, you don't want to," he added silkily.

Indecision tore at her. If she rearranged her schedule, she could just possibly squeeze him in. But did she want to? He wanted her today, at that particular point in time, but she had no guarantees of how long that would last. If she weren't so vulnerable at that moment, if she hadn't suffered his indifference once before, she wouldn't be so gun-shy. As it was, she just couldn't risk another heartache. "You've got no right to show up here and start pressuring me," she snapped.

"I have every right," he told her smoothly. "And I'm not putting pressure on you." With two long strides he eliminated the distance between them, a dawning awareness breaking over his face. "Is that what this is all about? Are you afraid of me?"

"Of course not," she denied quickly, perching on the edge of her chair anxiously. No, she wasn't afraid of him. It was her own treacherous body she feared. When he was near, his needs, his desires, became hers, and she no longer had control of her own destiny. "Cameron, surely you can see that this would never work," she began in a shaky voice. "The first rule I made when I established the company was that employees are not allowed to become romantically involved with the clients they work with. If that happens, the employee is immediately switched to another client. So you see, I can't do something I won't let my employees do. You want to become involved—"

"We *are* involved," he interrupted huskily. "But you don't need to be afraid of me. I told you last week I wasn't going to rush you into bed, and I meant it."

Suddenly, Cameron moved around behind her. Blair could feel the heat of his body scorching her back. When she jumped in sudden panic, his hands fastened around her waist. "Easy, sweetheart," he murmured. "There's no need to be jumpy."

Blair tried to ignore his hot breath in her ear, the thunderous pounding of her heart, her shortness of breath, but she failed miserably. She was surrounded by him, and the quaking his closeness generated in her threatened to erupt at any moment. She had to stop this madness before it went any further. "What are you doing?" she choked. "Anyone could walk in. . . ."

"No one will. Caroline will see to that." He tried to draw her back against his chest and laughed softly when she stubbornly pulled away and inched closer to the edge of the chair. He followed. "Sweetheart, I'm just trying to reassure you."

She snorted. "Is that what you call this?"

"Yes." His arms slid up her arms, and Blair gasped at the unexpected rush of sensation this small gesture aroused.

"If you'd just let me explain what I would expect from you if you accepted me as a client, you'd see you have nothing to fear," Cameron continued.

"You can explain without being quite so close," she gasped.

"I could, but it wouldn't feel nearly as nice." His fingers closed around her hand to bring it to his mouth. With the gentle persuasion of his lips and tongue, he began a languorous exploration of each finger, sensually testing and learning the feel of her skin, the shape of her hand. When his tongue dipped into her palm, she gasped and he repeated the caress. Blair trembled and closed her eyes to more fully savor the effervescence of desire that drugged her resistance.

"First of all," he spoke against her palm, "your duties wouldn't include touching me. You would never have to do this"—he licked at the pounding pulse in her wrist—"or this"—he closed all her fingers except the index finger, which he slowly guided around his mouth.

Blair felt her insides melt to warm honey, any thoughts of resistance overcome by a sweet lassitude she couldn't summon the strength to fight. His tongue made gentle forays down the length of each finger, always coming back to her palm, the pure sensuality of his touch too potent to ignore. With a sigh she relaxed against him. She should pull her hand free, but she couldn't—not just yet. She leaned her head against his shoulder and looked up at him to whisper through suddenly dry lips, "Touching clients is strictly against the rules."

He watched her lips form every word. "And what about kissing? Is that against the rules?"

She opened her mouth to answer and found her words swallowed by his waiting mouth. He gave her no time to protest, no chance to retreat. His arms closed around her and turned her body more fully toward him until she was practically sprawled against him. The rising heat in his body called to an answering need in hers that sparked to life and threatened to inflame them both.

This was not the teasing kiss he had tortured her with a week earlier. He took bold possession of her mouth, his teeth tugging at her lower lip gently, incessantly, stoking flames of passion that she had long since thought cold. She offered herself to him willingly, leaning into him enticingly, seductively. In a lazy and wholly satisfying way he explored the secret recesses of her mouth until Blair was breathless. When Cameron tore his mouth free, she collapsed against him weakly. "Yes," she gasped in a voice she hardly recognized as her own.

He lifted an eyebrow. "Yes what?" He grinned.

"Yes, kissing is against the rules." But how could anything this right be against the rules? she wondered idly.

"Then there's nothing to worry about, is there?" His satisfied, almost smug tone warned her she must have missed something. She frowned and he quickly explained. "If you're afraid of accepting me as a client, you have nothing to worry about. Touching you," he whispered, his hand moving to cover her breast in gentle possession, "and kissing you," he said against her lips, "is against the rules."

Blair stared at him dumbly. "I didn't mean..."

A quick knock shattered their private world, and before Blair could move out of his intimate hold, Caroline burst into the room. "Blair, I'm sorry to disturb you, but—" she glanced up from the papers she was holding and stopped in her tracks. "Oops! Don't mind me, folks. I'm just passing through."

"Caroline, wait!" Blair struggled to shake off the passion-filled fog that had snatched her from reality for those few precious moments, and glanced angrily at Cameron. How had he ever got her into this position?

"What's it going to be, Blair?" he asked her, his grin wicked. "Are you going to accept me as a client or not? Believe me, I'm prepared to stay here as long as it takes to get you to agree to this."

Caroline stood in the doorway, a huge grin on her face, and Blair could have cheerfully kicked them both. Unfortunately she wasn't in the position to do anything except give in as graciously as her temper would allow. "Yes, damn you! Now, let go of me!"

He did, albeit reluctantly. When she scrambled to her feet, he winked at the woman still standing in the doorway. "Thanks, Caroline. Your timing was perfect."

"Any time," she said, smiling.

Cameron got to his feet smoothly, grinning as Blair hastily stepped out of his reach. "Come over tomorrow night and fix dinner. We can work out a schedule then."

A slow burn began in her midsection and spread like wildfire. She could practically feel her blood boiling. How dare he give her orders! "Are you asking me or telling me?" she asked silkily.

He opened his mouth to answer but thought better of it. He grinned guilelessly. "I'm asking you, but forget I asked. I'll take you out instead and we can discuss it over dinner." He saw the refusal forming on her lips and quickly said, "I know you're going to be busy, but you've got to eat, so you may as well eat with me."

A crowded restaurant was infinitely safer than the dangerous privacy of his apartment. If she had learned anything since his return to Boston, it was that she was just as sensitive to his touch as she had always been, and her chances of denying her body's natural responses were about as good as the odds on her piloting the next space shuttle. For her own peace of mind she had to avoid the temptation of being alone with him. "All right, I'll go."

After agreeing to pick her up around seven, he left, and with his leave-taking, the office echoed with a tense silence. Blair lifted accusing eyes to her best friend. "Did you really help him set that up? How could you? You know what I went through after the divorce. How could you deliberately encourage—"

"Whoa, hold it," Caroline interrupted, realization dawning in her eyes. "I had nothing to do with any of this. In case you didn't notice, I was pretty stunned to walk in here and find you in his arms. Why didn't you tell me you were planning a reconciliation?"

"Because we're not." Blair sank back into the chair behind her desk and tried to ignore the masculine scent that lingered around her. She sighed wearily. "Cameron is the one who's planning things, not I. He claims the divorce was a mistake."

"And how do you feel about that?"

"I don't know. He's so damn persuasive! I want to believe him, but—"

"You don't want to get hurt again," her friend guessed. "You take a risk every time you love someone, Blair. You know that. You've got to decide if Cameron is worth the risk." Her eyes twinkled mischievously. "Personally I think he's worth it. If I weren't so crazy about Mike, Cameron wouldn't have a snowball's chance in hell of getting away from me."

She slapped the papers she was holding down on Blair's desk. "Here's Susan Clark's application. She's waiting to be interviewed."

- 4 -

A BURST OF laughter floated on the air to drown out temporarily the clatter of silverware and the steady hum of conversation. Blair leaned back against the bottle-green upholstery and smiled, hugging the sound to herself. How she had missed this place. Her eyes swept the brass and mahogany decor of the Back Bay Restaurant, touching on the long bar with the brass rail that had propped up many a foot, lingering on the shadowy corner she and Cameron had made their own special place. He had asked her to marry him there. Thank God he'd had the sensitivity to avoid that particular table tonight. She hadn't been there in ages. After the divorce she'd found herself standing in front of the double-paned doors many times, but the mixture of laughter and her own bittersweet memories had mocked her loneliness, and she'd never made it inside. Even now she couldn't forget that this was always the first place she and Cameron would come to when he returned from an assignment—after, that is, they slaked their too-long-denied passion for each other.

"What are you thinking about?"

She blinked and dragged her eyes back to the man seated across from her. Would there ever come a time when her heart wouldn't skip at the mere sight of him? Whenever she was near him, her eyes couldn't seem to get enough of him. They roamed at will over his broad shoulders, her blood racing at the way his black crew-neck sweater matched the bottomless depths of his eyes. Dark and mysterious, his hair swept back casually to brush the collar of the white shirt he wore beneath the sweater, he had attracted the attention of every female in the restaurant, and Blair was no exception. He looked marvelous in black.

"Blair?" He leaned forward and waved his hand in front of her face, mischievous laughter teasing his mouth, his eyes burning brightly as they leisurely inspected her peach-colored crepe blouse, which rose softly with each breath she took. "Come back to earth, honey."

Heat licked at her senses, singeing her cheeks, cutting off her breath. Hastily she reached for her water glass and took a quick swallow, although she was still unbearably hot. Her eyes met his before quickly skirting away. "Sorry," she said huskily. "I was just thinking of the past—and all the many times we came here...."

He reached across the table to still her nervous movements, his dark eyes soft with teasing laughter. "And why would that make you blush?"

She longed to put her hands to her face, to hide her traitorous skin from his all seeing eyes. But what was the use? He had been a reporter for too many years, and he knew her like a book anyway. Would she ever be able to read him so easily? His enigmatic face concealed his most private thoughts and allowed her to see only what he wanted her to see. And right now, more than anything, she needed to know what he really wanted from her.

"I'm not blushing. My cheeks are chapped from the wind." She tugged her hand free of his and placed it out of reach in her lap, jerkily picking at a strand of invisible lint that clung to her tan wool pants. "Don't you think it's time we got down to business?" she asked abruptly. "You didn't

Made in Heaven

want to talk until after dinner. We've eaten, so talk."

"You're determined to keep this on a business level, aren't you?" he accused in exasperation. "Every time the conversation comes close to being personal, you shy away like a scared rabbit."

"I do not!"

"I can understand how you feel. But you can't keep it up, sweetheart. My patience isn't inexhaustible. One day soon you're going to have to confront what we have together."

But what do we have? She stared at him in frustration. They'd had three years of hellos and good-byes, followed by two years of emptiness. The passion, the desire, that they sparked in each other offered little consolation against the reality of day-to-day living. It didn't seem to matter how much they wanted each other if Cameron was off in his own little world of ink and by-lines and remembered her presence only at intervals. He was there now, but for how long? She refused to lay her heart on the line again just so he could step on it on his way up the ladder to success.

"What nights do you need me?" she asked stubbornly.

"Every night, but I don't suppose you'd agree to that." When she only glared at him, he sighed. "How about Wednesdays, Fridays, and Sundays?"

She nodded stiffly. "That shouldn't be any problem. What specific services do you need?" His eyes twinkled at her question. She ground her teeth in frustration and snapped, "You know what I mean, Cameron. Just what exactly do you expect me to do three nights a week?"

"Obviously not what you're thinking," he chuckled, "but I'm willing to be persuaded." When she made a move to grab her purse and slide out of the booth, he reached across the table and stopped her by simply touching her arm. "Hey, I was only kidding. What happened to your sense of humor?"

"I lost it." And could she have used it now! If she could just laugh it off, he'd never touch her heart.

Somber awareness suddenly made him grim. "Am I wasting my time? Did I hurt you so badly that you can't stand the sight of me?"

"No! I . . . I don't know." She didn't know anything any more. "I'm so confused right now, I don't know how I feel," she admitted honestly.

"Don't you think you should give yourself some time, then?" he suggested. "Accept me as a client. I'll expect no more from you than any other client. I promise. All I really need you to do is cook dinner for me three nights a week. And stay and keep me company while I eat."

She eyed him warily. "That's all it would involve?"

"That and keeping an open mind." He grabbed her hand, his thumb absently caressing her skin. "The decision we made two years ago was a mistake. We belong together, honey. Give us a chance."

How could she deny him? Or herself? "All right," she sighed. "As long as you understand that I'm only agreeing to cook you dinner. I'm not dessert."

He grinned and reached for her coat, signaling that it was time to leave. "It's a deal."

Two days later Blair sat at the kitchen table, her sandy hair neatly coiled at the nape of her neck, her petite figure encased in a white silk blouse and teal blue split skirt, gloom on her face. Morosely she stared at the copper teakettle that sang merrily on the stove, watching it fill the old-fashioned kitchen with steam. Was there a sign, a blinding flash of light, that would tell her if there was any point in trying to rekindle a fire from the ashes of her love for Cameron? she mused. There had to be a point when hope turned into hopelessness, but so far her traitorous heart refused to recognize it. Cameron was determined to reestablish himself in her life, and he was succeeding more than he realized. He dropped by at the most unexpected times, delighting Julie and destroying her own carefully maintained equilibrium. She found herself thinking of him at the most inappropriate times. Her skin burned at the thought of his persuasive touch on the day he came to her office. He hadn't touched her since except in the most casual of ways, but he had made no secret of his desire for her. She had seen the longing in his eyes, and the confidence. He was going to bide his time and, in the process, drive her quietly out of her mind. She found herself tottering on the edge of anticipation every time he came within her line of vision, and it was exquisite torture.

"Earth to Blair. Earth to Blair. Come in, please," Caroline called, snapping her fingers just inches from Blair's nose.

Blair jerked back to attention, grinning sheepishly, her eyes once again focusing on the four women seated around her kitchen table for coffee and doughnuts and the biweekly staff meeting. "Sorry about that," she said, laughing softly. "I was thinking about something else." She really had to quit wandering off like that. "What were we talking about?"

"Doug Stinson," Gina Jones said dreamily.

Blair chuckled and turned to the oldest of her four employees. "How are you making out with our famous baseball pitcher, Carla?" At the titter of laughter that greeted her words, she laughed. "Maybe I should rephrase that. Are you having any problems?"

"Only one," Carla replied promptly. "How do I adopt a grown man?"

"I don't know why you get such a good-looking hunk," Gina grumbled good-naturedly. "You can bet if I had him, I wouldn't want to adopt him."

"Which is precisely why he's not your client," Blair retorted bluntly, the teasing sparkle in her eyes robbing her words of sting. "When he made inquiries about Maid-In-Heaven, he wasn't even sure he wanted a 'wife.' It's always open season on professional athletes, and he had every reason to be leery of inviting a strange woman into his home. The last thing he needs is to come home to find his 'wife' *in* the bed instead of making it."

"Come on, Blair, you know I wouldn't do that."

"No, but Carla was still the right choice for Doug."

To ensure the success of Maid-In-Heaven, it was essential that Blair match each client with just the right "wife." It was not an undertaking she took lightly. Each of her four employees had different specialties, and it was Blair's job to capitalize on their individual expertise. When Doug Stinson, a pitcher for the Boston Red Sox, approached her, she knew Carla Knight was the only one for the job. A card-carrying senior citizen, Carla posed no threat to the young bachelor. She was a motherly woman, widowed, and truly loved looking after what she termed her "boys." Blair suspected she spoiled all her clients rotten—and that they loved every minute of it.

Gina Jones, on the other hand, was a striking woman in her mid-twenties whose poise and unconscious sexuality would have overwhelmed Doug Stinson. She was an excellent hostess, however, and her cooking skills were legendary. She was in great demand among the executive clients who entertained frequently.

Blair checked the legal pad on which she had jotted a few notes for the meeting. She loved these get-togethers with her employees, but she knew they couldn't continue to meet in her kitchen indefinitely. The business was expanding and soon the staff would be too large for such small quarters. She would have to rent an office downtown. Blair sighed. She would miss the cozy informality. "And how about you, Teri?" she asked the youngest member of the group, who had been unusually quiet. "You've been working for Mr. Clawson about a month now. Is everything going smoothly? No complaints?"

"Well..." Teri's slim fingers closed around her coffee cup to grip it tightly, her gray eyes as dark and brooding as a winter's day. "There's only one little problem: I can't work tonight." Before Blair could start to question her, she rushed on with an explanation. "I know I'm not giving you much notice, but I didn't know until today. My brother's flying in this afternoon to see me before he takes off for Europe tomorrow. I haven't seen him for six months, and I was hoping I could get someone to take over for me." She looked around the table anxiously.

Silence reigned. "What are your duties tonight?" Blair asked finally when it looked as though no one was going to come to the girl's rescue.

"Just cooking a small dinner for two." Disappointment was already weighing on Teri's slim shoulders. "Mr. Clawson doesn't even want me to serve. I was going to cook everything this afternoon so he could heat it up later in the microwave. It's only a couple of hours of work at the most."

"I'd really like to help you out," Caroline said regretfully, "but there's no way I can fit in another job today. I'm overbooked already."

Gina wrinkled her nose. "Mrs. Pittman's having a Christmas party tonight, and she'd have a fit if I wasn't there to supervise things in the kitchen. She can be a real pain in the neck sometimes, but I did promise. If you needed me tomorrow, there'd be no problem."

"Carla?" Blair asked hopefully.

The older woman shook her head. "I'm sorry. I've got a dozen errands that have to be run this afternoon, plus a doctor's appointment. And you know how that is. I could be tied up there anywhere from thirty minutes to two hours."

Blair found all eyes focused on her and knew with a sinking feeling that there was no way she could turn Teri down. "What time does Mr. Clawson want dinner?"

"Anytime after six-thirty," Teri replied promptly. "Are you going to take over for me, Blair?"

"You don't think I'm going to let you miss seeing your brother, do you? Anyway, it shouldn't cause any problems. It's my night to cook dinner for Cameron, but he's coming here to the house so he'll have more time to spend with Julie. He'll understand if I'm a little late."

"If he doesn't, it'll be no more than you deserve," Caroline teased. "I distinctly remember hearing you say we weren't taking on any more clients until the first of the year."

Blair blushed. "You know I have a hard time saying no to Cameron."

"I'll be sure to tell him. He'll be glad to hear it."

Late that afternoon Blair struggled into Kenneth Clawson's house with an armload of groceries and a wok, mercilessly berating herself. How had she ever got herself into this mess? The small dinner for two that Kenneth Clawson was expecting tonight was, in fact, a complete Oriental dinner. He had even given Teri recipes of the dishes he wanted prepared, and there wasn't a canned or frozen food on the list.

Grumbling to herself, Blair found her way into the kitchen and began unpacking the groceries, her movements the only sound in the otherwise still house. If she hustled, she just might make it back to her own house without being excessively late. Casting an anxious eye at the clock, she quickly combined the ingredients for steamed ginger buns.

A myriad hummingbirds took flight in her stomach as her thoughts turned to Cameron. He didn't need Caroline to tell him that Blair had a weakness for him. He had always known it. Even though he was less than sure of her right now, he had counted on her continued feelings for him in pressing her to accept him as a client. He didn't know that he had conspired with that small ray of hope that she hadn't been able to banish from her heart, and she couldn't turn her back on him, although reason urged her to do just that.

The painful lessons she had learned from him, however, were not discarded. Even though she longed to throw caution to the winds and welcome him back into her life, her arms, she couldn't. A part of her—the all-too-vulnerable essence of her being—stood back warily, reluctant to believe that his current interest in her would prove any more lasting than his interest had the first time. She had grown cynical, perhaps out of self-preservation, and she didn't need to remind herself that once before his pursuit had overwhelmed her. His interest had quickly waned, though, when work rushed in to distract him. Was he simply replaying a very old song that could only end one way?

Setting the dough aside to rise, she mixed the dressing for the Chinese garden salad and put it in the refrigerator to chill. Was she overreacting, overstating the need to protect herself from Cameron's fatal charm? In all fairness she had to admit that he was just as anxious as she to avoid another mistake. He was moving slowly, as he had promised, and she didn't know if she loved him or hated him for that. The loneliness of the past rose up to envelop her, and she found herself wanting to run to him, to escape her

Made in Heaven

haunting memories. It was times like these that terrified her. The hours, the years, she had fought her own yearnings were meaningless, of no more importance than the blink of an eye. She was horribly afraid she was slipping backward, and utilizing all her instincts toward survival, she shored up her sagging defenses and vainly tried to quell her throbbing emotions. She would not spend every waking and sleeping moment thinking of Cameron Wakefield.

Methodically she cut the beef, mushrooms, and green onions in preparation for stir-frying. Once the ginger buns had been placed in the wok to steam, she set the table and began to assemble the ingredients for the fruit with the sesame sauce that would end the meal. She checked the items off in her head as she lined them up before her. Strawberries, oranges, honey, sesame seeds. Where were the sesame seeds? She knew she had bought them. She distinctly remembered placing the small jar in the shopping cart. In growing panic she searched the cupboards and counter with one eye on the clock and finally had to admit that the grocery clerk must have forgotten to put them in the sack. "Damn!" So much for her plans to be out of here by six-thirty. She couldn't possibly finish cooking the rest of the meal, go to the grocery store, finish the dessert, and have dinner ready by the time Cameron arrived at the house. She was definitely running late.

In a burst of frenzied activity Blair rushed around the kitchen, unable to explain even to herself why she was so anxious not to keep Cameron waiting. The beef was cooked, the salad prepared, and the fruit assembled, waiting only for the whipped cream, honey, and sesame seeds that would be combined deliciously as a topping. Making one last check to assure herself everything else was in order, she grabbed her coat and hurried out the door.

Everything seemed to conspire against her—the traffic, other shoppers, the cashier. By the time she returned to Kenneth Clawson's Elizabethan-style home, she was gnashing her teeth in frustration. After placing her coat over a kitchen chair, she quickly tied on her apron and began mixing the topping for the dessert. With swift, sure movements she dolloped the topping onto the fruit and placed her creation in the refrigerator. If she hurried, she'd be only thirty minutes late. Grinning wryly, she pushed back a strand of hair that had escaped the coil at her neck. The "wife" Cameron saw tonight would be slightly frazzled....

"Damn Joe Barker! He stole that contract from me. The bastard! And it was my turn to make the low bid," an angry male voice growled.

Blair, in the process of slipping into her coat, froze, her eyes drawn to the door that separated the kitchen from the dining room. She recognized Kenneth Clawson's voice almost immediately. "Last month he took that city contract right out from under Jerry McPherson's nose. I knew we shouldn't have trusted him."

"Something's got to be done," the other man replied, "before he puts us all out of business. He's going to steal one bid too many and someone is going to start wondering why he always makes the lowest bid."

The men's voices grew louder as they moved closer to the kitchen door, effectively snapping Blair out of the daze that had held her motionless. She snatched up her purse and quickly let herself out the back door.

"Well, hell!" she muttered irritably as she got in her car and pulled away from the curb. So much for her culinary skills. Kenneth Clawson and his guest were so upset, they probably wouldn't even taste the food she had spent the last two hours cooking. How could they appreciate homemade ginger buns when all they could think of were contracts and stolen bids? A frown worried her brow. And just what kind of shady deals were Kenneth Clawson and his dinner guest involved in, anyway?

The blare of a horn caused her to jerk to attention, and she hastily guided her car back into the lane from which it had begun to wander. The streets of Boston were no place to lose her concentration. Otherwise friendly, courteous Bostonians turned into ruthless fiends when placed behind the wheels of cars. If she wanted to get home in one piece, she would have to keep her mind on her driving.

When she reached the relative safety of her own house,

she shut the door behind her and collapsed against it. Home at last! Now, if she could only relax in a hot tub, she'd be in heaven.

Little footsteps thundered into the room as Julie hurled herself at her mother, her brown eyes star-spangled and impish dimples dancing in her cheeks. "Mama! Anna let me make cookies!"

"She did?" Blair exclaimed with a grin, teasingly flicking at the cookie crumbs clinging to her daughter's mouth. "Are you sure you didn't put more in your mouth than you did in the oven?"

"No," Julie giggled. "I couldn't eat *that* many."

"She only had two," Anna explained from the doorway; at seventeen, Anna was a younger version of her mother, Caroline. "And she snuck those when I wasn't looking. I hope it won't ruin her appetite."

Blair ruffled her daughter's chestnut curls. "It'd take more than two cookies to do that." She handed the girl the money she owed her. "Thanks, Anna. I'm sorry I was late."

"That's okay," she said, shrugging off the apology and zipping up her navy wool jacket. "I enjoyed it." She gave Julie's hair a playful tug. "I'll see you tomorrow, squirt."

Dreams of a long, hot soak in the tub vanished as the grandfather clock in the foyer struck seven. Blair's fingers fumbled with her coat. "We've got to hurry, honey. Daddy will be here soon and I haven't even started dinner."

"Do I get to cook?" Julie asked, wide-eyed.

"Well, you can help," Blair amended. Critically she eyed the limp white blouse she had worn all day. It was definitely beginning to look the worse for wear, but she just didn't have time to change. With a grimace she headed for the kitchen and an apron. "You can set the table," she told the little girl who followed in her wake. "Do you remember how?"

"Of course," Julie replied indignantly. "I can do it, Mama."

Blair bit her lip. "I beg your pardon," she teased. Julie was at the stage where she wanted to do everything for herself, from tying her shoes to cutting her meat. Her struggle for independence was at times trying but, more often than not, amusing. Chuckling to herself, Blair began preparing steaks for the broiler.

"Is Santa coming tonight?" Julie asked hopefully as Blair tossed a salad. "Do you know Santa, Mama? Daddy does."

Blair grinned. "Yes, I know Santa. And no, he's not coming tonight."

"Daddy's going to take me to see him. And I can ask him for *anything* I want."

"But you have to be a good girl," her mother warned her. "Santa watches you all the time, and he only brings presents to good kids."

Julie's slim, childish brows drew together in puzzlement. "How can he see me?"

"Good question, sweetheart. How can he see her, Mama?"

The masculine chuckle warmed her blood, and she glanced up to find Cameron standing in the kitchen doorway, a crooked grin softening the hard angles of his face, his eyes flaring with dark fires. He wore a wine-colored sweater and gray corduroy slacks with an easy grace that was totally relaxed and wickedly sexy. Blair felt her senses respond to him and had to make a conscious effort to quell the sudden urge to walk right into his arms. Dear Lord, what was wrong with her? Color rushed to her cheeks, and she frantically searched for something, anything, to bank the flames sparking to life inside her. "You tell us. You're the one who knows Santa."

"It's a secret," he whispered loudly in Julie's ear, grinning at her giggles. "I promised not to tell."

"Oh, Daddy, please," Julie pleaded. "I won't tell."

"But Santa would know I told," he replied promptly, mischief gleaming in his eyes. "No, I couldn't break my promise."

Blair placed the salad on the table and turned to find him right behind her. Her heart lurched painfully. "Are you hungry?"

"Actually I'm starved," Cameron said huskily. His eyes slid over her, heating her blood, raising her blood pressure to dangerous heights. He held her captive with the sensuous curve of his lips, coming to a stop within inches of her. He looked at Julie. "It looks like it's time to eat, sweetheart. Go wash your hands."

"With soap," Blair called after her in a husky voice, tearing her eyes away from Cameron to meticulously straighten the silverware Julie had haphazardly arranged on the table. She took deep, steadying breaths and tried to still the hammering of her heart, but when Cameron ran his fingers down her cheek, her efforts were wasted. Her senses clamored with renewed awareness, and she jerked away, startled.

"You know it isn't food I hunger for," he murmured.

And how she knew! Suddenly the sexual tension crackling like electrical sparks between them was more than she could stand. She stepped back, out of reach. "I told you once before I wouldn't be dessert," she said tightly, her eyes locking with his. "And I meant it. If you're going to break our agreement, we can end things here and now, and you can go out for dinner."

"I wasn't breaking our agreement," he snapped impatiently. "Damn it, Blair, I'm not a robot! Can't I even touch you?"

"No," she whispered hoarsely. "Not yet." On shaky legs she turned from him, her clenched fists jammed into her apron pockets. How long could she continue this touch-me-touch-me-not game they were playing? He was determined to have her; it was only a matter of time, and she was horrified to discover that she was growing just as anxious as he. The hurt she had borne as a shield since the breakup of their marriage was offering less and less protection. She was dangerously close to forgetting everything but her need for him. Go slowly, go slowly! her heart cried, but she knew she was fighting a losing battle. Her heart had long since assured Cameron's victory.

The meal went smoothly, with Julie's bright chatter covering up the patches of silence that frequently stretched between Cameron and Blair. She asked innumerable questions, which they patiently answered, and gradually the tension eased. When Julie once again brought up the subject of Santa, Cameron suggested, "Would you like to go see Santa after we eat?"

"Can we?" Julie squealed, her eyes glowing. "And Mama, too?"

"Of course," he replied. "We wouldn't leave her here by herself."

Blair wanted to strangle him, but she waited until Julie ran to get her coat before turning to him with snapping eyes. "Please, Cameron! We agreed to my cooking dinner and keeping you company while you eat. But that's all we agreed to. I won't let you use Julie to tie up my evening."

"Is that what you think I was doing?" he growled.

"Weren't you?" She glared at him.

"For your information, I ceased being your client the minute we finished eating." He pushed away from the table to tower over her, irritation narrowing his eyes. "I'm asking you, Blair Wakefield, my ex-wife, not my rent-a-wife, if you would like to accompany Julie and me. I thought you might like to go out and relax for a while and leave business at home. Obviously I was mistaken."

"No..." Mortification curled her toes. He was only trying to be thoughtful, and she had jumped down his throat without even waiting for an explanation. "Cameron, I'm sorry. I shouldn't have snapped at you. I just didn't want you to get the wrong impression about our relationship."

"I'm not the one with the wrong impression," he replied pointedly. "Will you come with us or not?"

"I guess I will," she said slowly.

He grinned. "Let's go before you change your mind."

At the mall Julie climbed onto Santa's lap and regaled him with her dreams of owning a puppy. Cameron's arm slid around Blair as they stood watching their daughter, and Blair found herself leaning against him, unable to deny herself the closeness of the moment. His arm tightened. "You've done a terrific job with Julie. It must have been hard for you."

Blair looked up at him, surprised by the almost envious tone of his words. He knew what he had missed; she could see it reflected in his face. Regret saddened his eyes and she rushed to dispel it. "At times it was hard. But I always knew you'd be here if she really needed you."

"But that's not much good in the everyday scheme of things."

"She always knew where you were and why you couldn't be with her," Blair assured him earnestly. "I wanted her to know you and I think I succeeded. She's very comfortable with you."

He grinned wryly and pointed to his lips. "If you want to kiss it and make it better, you can plant one right here."

"Oh, no," she laughed, slipping free of his encircling arm. "That would be breaking the rules." Before he could reach for her again, she turned to find Julie skipping toward them; her hair was braided into a long plait that bounced with every step, a wide grin lighting her face. Blair gave her a swift hug. "Did you tell Santa everything you wanted?"

Julie nodded. "He said I've been a very good girl. He's been watching me."

"See. I told you," Cameron chuckled, scooping her up in his arms and heading for the car. "We'd better get you home. It's past your bedtime."

"Oh, Daddy, no!" Julie wailed. "I don't want to go to bed."

"Santa can see you," he warned, and then laughed when she admitted she was sleepy.

With Julie in the back seat, watching through sleepy eyes for the Christmas decorations lighting the dark night, they headed home. The guarded privacy of the front seat teased at Blair's sensitive nerves, and she knew she was much too aware of Cameron's closeness, his muscular thigh only inches from her own, his strong hands gripping the steering wheel. "How's work coming?" she blurted out. "Have you had any problems settling in?"

"It's been one nightmare after another," he admitted. "So far our advertising revenue is still too low, and that's really hurting us. And, of course, Stan is fighting us every step of the way. He's cut his rates way down, and we're having a hard time matching them."

"You can't really blame him."

"Hell, no, I don't blame him. I'd do the same thing if I were in his shoes. This is a cutthroat business."

"And are you going to fight fire with fire?" She waited patiently for his answer, knowing it before he gave it. Cameron was a winner. He set his sights on a goal and purposefully plugged away at it until he achieved it. He didn't give up and she'd do well to remember that.

"If I have to," he said flatly. "But I'd rather put the *Gazette* back on its feet by establishing it as a quality newspaper. So we've got to throw out the sensational headlines and yellow journalism and get back to sound, unbiased reporting. It's going to take time and a lot of hard work."

Uneasiness stole over her. How many times had she heard him talk about his work that way? He loved the smell of printer's ink, and clatter of the presses, the challenge of deadlines. How could she ever hope to compete with that?

All her joy in the evening fled and she cursed herself for her own foolishness. She couldn't hide from reality any longer, although it had been a delightful interlude. She had the instincts of a homing pigeon, while Cameron was a jungle cat. She wanted, needed, the comfort of her own fireside. Cameron, on the other hand, would never be happy unless he was prowling that jungle, staking out his own territory, ruling it. How could she ever have thought he'd changed?

When he parked in front of the house, the silence in the car was suddenly thick with expectation. Blair glanced over her shoulder to find Julie nodding in the back seat and hurriedly jumped at this excuse to escape. "Julie is worn out. I'd better get her up to bed."

"I'll carry her," Cameron offered. With a minimum of motion he was out of the car and easily lifting Julie in his arms.

The sting of tears suddenly burned her eyes and Blair had to fumble with the key for several revealing seconds before she was able to unlock the door. She was a sentimental idiot for letting him get to her like this. Seeing him with Julie nestled trustingly in his arms should be a familiar sight to her, but it wasn't, dammit! They should have done this a thousand times, but they hadn't. The sharing, the special closeness of family life, had been denied them, lost in the winds of ambition that had swept Cameron away from them, away from her. Regardless of what they managed to salvage of the future, they could never go back.

Avoiding Cameron's watchful eyes, she hurried up the stairs to Julie's room and pulled back the covers of her bed. For the next few minutes she concentrated on changing her limp daughter into her pajamas, and tried to pretend she wasn't aware of Cameron hovering in the doorway. When she could no longer delay going downstairs, she leaned over to kiss Julie tenderly on the forehead, then tried to squeeze past Cameron and into the hallway without touching him. She didn't succeed.

His arms came up the minute she was even with him, locking her within his loose embrace. When she stiffened, he frowned in puzzlement. "What's the matter?"

"Nothing," she replied shortly. "I'm just tired and I don't have time to wrestle with you."

One dark brow lifted dangerously. "I didn't realize we were wrestling," he said softly, thoughtfully. "But maybe that's what we have been doing."

Anxious to avoid an analysis of their relationship, she quickly asked, "Do you have any plans for the next couple of hours?"

"Only to spend them with you."

His words were sheathed in velvet, and Blair shied from them like a frightened mare. She skittishly broke his hold on her and stepped into the hall, her movements stiff, her breath coming in agitated gulps. "Would you mind spending them with Julie instead? I've got shopping to do, and the stores are open late tonight."

Impatience flickered in Cameron's eyes as he took two long strides to catch up with her as she hurried down the hall. "Can't that wait? I was hoping we'd have a chance to talk."

She shook her head. "Sorry. I've just got too much to do. This is the busiest time of the year for me, and I've got to keep to my schedule."

His impatience quickly gave way to anger when she hurried down the stairs and searched her purse for her keys.

"You're really going to do this? Walk out on me to go shopping for a bunch of lazy bachelors who should be doing their own Christmas shopping?"

"Didn't you let me do all the shopping for your family when we were married?" she demanded, angered by his tone. How dare he belittle her business! "That's one of the wifely services you were quick to take advantage of," she continued.

Cameron flushed. "I can think of a lot of 'wifely services' I need more than shopping."

"I am not your wife!"

"Well, you damn well ought to be!"

"And whose fault is it that I'm not?" she asked reproachfully. "Having a wife didn't seem all that important to you two years ago. You didn't think twice about dropping everything, including me, to go gallivanting off to Europe."

"Blair, I was working."

"I know." She sighed wearily. "You were always working." She pulled open the door and glanced over her shoulder, her face stiff with the effort not to give way completely to the hurt that throbbed deep inside. "I'll be back in a couple of hours."

Her last impression as she shut the door was of the frustration etched on his face. No doubt Cameron was furious at her stubborn insistence on dredging up the past, but she couldn't just cover it up and forget it. She would *never* forget the wrenching loneliness that had torn her apart when he left without her. How many times had she reached for him in the night, only to find her arms holding emptiness? How many times had she walked into the study, the living room, the bedroom, expecting to see him, only to find herself alone? Until she could get beyond those memories, beyond that pain, she couldn't let him penetrate the most vulnerable depths of her heart.

When she returned home hours later, laden down with packages, her tired feet groaning with every step she took, the past was safely stored away in the cool reserve that straightened her spine and lifted her chin. She found Cameron reading in the living room, a memory come to life.

Made in Heaven 73

Her steps wavered for a minute, but she ruthlessly forced herself to continue walking into the room. She dumped her packages haphazardly on the couch. He looked up from the book he was reading, his face as impassive as her own. "Did you get everything you needed? You look like you bought out the store."

"Just about." She stared at the fire jumping in the fireplace until the silence between them was stretched taut. She could feel his eyes on her, brooding and resentful, but dammit, he didn't own her! He had no right to lay claim to her time—to lay claim to her. She glared at him. "Would you like me to do some shopping for you? Since you *are* a client—"

"No! I don't want to be labeled another one of your lazy bachelors."

"I never said my clients were lazy," she objected stiffly.

With breathtaking quickness he moved to her side, impatiently pushing packages out of the way and grabbing her hands. *"Don't,"* he stressed fiercely, "group me with the rest of your clients. You're shutting me out and I don't like it. It's driving me crazy!"

She stared at him with wide, tortured eyes, his closeness battling with the turmoil that twisted her heart into knots. She felt battered and bruised from the constant struggle, and she couldn't hide the pain a second longer. "I won't let you hurt me again!" she cried. "I couldn't stand it!"

He swore softly and jerked her into his arms. "God, sweetheart, I'm not trying to hurt you. I'm just trying to get past this damn wall you've built around yourself. Every time I think I'm getting close, I run into it. I don't know what I can do to convince you I've changed. I'm not my father, Blair."

She wanted to believe him. But for as long as she had known him, he had been possessed by the same all-consuming ambition and drive that had pulled his father into a world of success that had no place for family, wives, or lovers. Could he have changed that much? She didn't even dare to hope. "I know you're not your father. I want to believe you, but I can't pretend I do. In fact, just the thought of getting close to you scares me half to death," she blurted, surprising herself with her honesty.

"This isn't easy for me either," he admitted roughly. He lifted her chin to stare deep into her eyes, searching out her innermost feelings. "You know, lady, you've got pretty high expectations. I don't know if I can live up to them, but at least give me a chance." When she started to speak, he touched her lips with his fingers and the words died in her throat. "Trust me, honey, just trust me."

How she wanted to! "I'm trying," she said huskily.

The laugh lines at the corners of his eyes deepened as he smiled wryly and released her. "That's all I can ask. And before I forget my good intentions, I'm going to get out of here." He came to his feet and strode quickly to the door. "Sleep tight, sweetheart."

An arctic wind whistled around the house several days later, and blowing snow darkened the day, echoing the chill that crept into Blair's heart. She shivered, her maroon cowl-neck sweater offering little warmth against a coldness that came from within. She sat at her desk, a troubled frown knitting her brow, and gently replaced the receiver on its cradle. Closing her eyes, she replayed in her head the entire conversation she had just had with Cameron, hoping against hope that she was simply jumping to conclusions.

"With the weather bad as it is, I think we should cancel dinner. It's only going to get worse tonight, and I'd feel better if I knew you and Julie were safe at home. I'll just fix myself a sandwich."

"I don't have to take Julie out," she objected. "I can probably get Anna to stay with her. But I'll come. I can't let a little snow interfere with the performance of my job."

"Will you forget the damn agreement we made!" he snapped. "I don't want you out in this kind of weather." At her stiff silence he sighed. "I'm sorry. It's been a long day, and it's going to be a while before it's over. Jack Trawick and I are meeting with some of the advertisers, and I'll probably be tied up for most of the evening anyway. So let's just cancel tonight. Okay?" When she didn't answer, he said sharply, "Blair? Are you still there?"

She swallowed the fear in her throat. "Yes."

He swore softly. "I called the meeting *after* I heard the weather report. If you don't believe me, say so," he exploded. "Rant and rave, throw a fit, but don't go icy on me or I swear I'll come over there and heat your blood so fast, it'll make your head spin. And don't think I can't do it."

Oh, he could do it, all right. And they both knew it. "If I'm upset, it's something I have to learn to deal with alone. If you don't need my services tonight, that's quite all right. I can certainly utilize the time. Good-bye."

Had he really canceled dinner because he was concerned for her safety? Or was he using that as an excuse so he could hold a business meeting? He wanted her to trust him, but it was very hard. They both had interests that pulled them away from their private lives. Where was the *Gazette* on Cameron's list of priorities? Where was she? Those were questions she couldn't readily answer.

The phone rang again almost immediately, and she stared at it hesitantly before snatching it up. "Maid-In-Heaven. May I help you?"

"I certainly hope so," Stan chuckled in her ear. "How about having dinner with a lonely bachelor? I'll make it worth your while."

Blair laughed and let the tension ease out of her. "Have you looked outside lately?"

"A little snow won't hurt you. What do you say? Is it a date?"

She grimaced at the client invoices spread out before her, reminding her of all the work she still had to do. "Really, Stan, I think I should stay home. I've got a few problems to straighten out, and Julie's been wanting to make Christmas cookies. Maybe another time?"

"All right," he said grudgingly, "but only because of Julie. What kind of problems are you having? No, let me guess: It's about six foot one, a hundred and ninety pounds, and stubborn as hell."

"How'd you guess? Is he giving you problems, too?"

"You might say that," he replied dryly. "He caught us

flat-footed when he bought the *Gazette*. We weren't prepared for the competition, and he's already starting to make inroads in our circulation. But I've still got a few tricks up my sleeve."

"Stan," she objected worriedly, "don't do anything that might destroy your friendship—"

"*I'm* not doing anything of that nature," he interrupted. "Cameron started all this, but I know you don't want to hear that, so let's just drop it. What other problems are you having?"

She looked at the invoice for Kenneth Clawson, vividly recalling the Chinese dinner she had cooked. "Oh, it's nothing. Just a problem with a client."

"Come on," he coaxed. "Tell Uncle Stan all about it. Maybe I can help."

"You always have before," she laughed. "I just don't know what to do. I overheard something at a client's the other day, and unless I was imagining things, the man is involved in a bid-rigging scheme. He's a contractor and—"

"What's his name?"

"Ken—" The intensity of his tone tripped an alarm, and she hastily swallowed the rest of Kenneth Clawson's name. "Why do you want to know?" she asked suspiciously.

"Why? Because it needs to be investigated, of course," he said impatiently. "There could be a great story here...."

"No! No, Stan! Don't you dare use this for a story!"

"But this could be important," he persisted.

"I have my own standards to maintain," she said heatedly. "Do you know what would happen to Maid-In-Heaven's reputation, if I betrayed the trust of one of my clients?"

"Don't worry," he assured her. "I'll keep you and Maid-In-Heaven out of it."

"You're darn right you will," she countered quickly, "because you're not going to pursue it. You can't, Stan. Promise me you won't. I was probably imagining the whole thing anyway. I was on my way out the door and I must have misunderstood."

He sighed heavily and Blair could picture him running

his fingers through his hair in frustration. "I'm not so sure about that. Maybe I should look into this."

"Believe me, Stan," she entreated him, "there's nothing to look into. My client was just mad because he got beat out of a contract he was sure he'd won. It probably happens all the time, so let's forget it. Okay?"

"Okay." Stan snorted in disgust. "But I still think there's more to this than you're telling me."

"And I think you're paranoid." She laughed in relief. "There's no story here."

- 5 -

BLAIR LAY STARING at the ceiling, the darkness of the night encompassing her until she was foundering in her own misery. She snuggled under the comforter, covering her bare shoulders, the black lace of her nightgown sliding over her legs to whisper seductively; yet, coldness still shadowed her heart. Where was Cameron? Was he lying in his own bed, sleepless because of her? He was probably still furious with her for not meekly accepting his cancellation of their appointment. Was she supposed to be happy because he had elected to spend the evening with a group of stuffy old men instead of her?

Why had she let him open the old wounds? she wondered with a dry sob. She had made a life for herself without him, and while she couldn't honestly say she was ecstatically happy, she was content. She had grown up at last, and in the process she had put away her adolescent fantasies and dreams. It wasn't easy, but she did it. Cameron, damn him, had destroyed all that. Dreams she had ruthlessly denied herself for two long years were suddenly upon her, mocking the voice of reason that warned her they were on paths going in opposite directions, two ships passing in the night without hope of calling the same port home. Would it take another lifetime to put him out of her heart this time?

The phone resting on the bedside table rang, shattering her musings. Startled, she reached for it, the sudden pounding of her heart shaking her fingers. She hated late-night phone calls. They invariably brought bad news, and right now she didn't need that. "Hello?"

"Did I wake you?" Cameron asked softly.

Tension flowed out of her, and she collapsed against the pillows. She closed her eyes. His voice in her ear was so real, so close, she could almost pretend he was there in bed with her. She swallowed the unexpected lump in her throat and said in a surprisingly steady voice, "No, I was just lying here, thinking."

"About me, I hope."

"As a matter of fact, I was," she replied.

"Blair, about this afternoon," he began almost defensively. "I was a first-class jackass and I'm sorry. I had no right to jump down your throat just because you didn't react the way I wanted you to."

"And how did you want me to react?"

"With understanding. Without suspicion of my motive."

She sighed. They were back to square one. "I did understand, but you can't blame me for being a little suspicious. Making excuses to stay at work can become a habit. I'm afraid you've slipped back into your old work habits without even realizing it."

"I didn't cancel dinner so I could work," he replied irritably. "But since the weather had already shot the evening to hell, I decided I might as well salvage some of it. These things happen."

Her fingers clutched the hard plastic of the receiver, but she hardly noticed. A sense of déjà vu swept over her, and fear threw open the door to all her resentment. "Are you trying to tell me I can expect more of this in the future?"

"Don't be ridiculous," he snapped. "Tonight was a fluke

and you're doing just what I was afraid you'd do—blowing it all out of proportion. Can't you see that I only canceled our plans because of my feelings for you?"

"And just what exactly are your feelings for me?"

"Do you really have to ask?" he said in surprise. "I could spend a lifetime or more telling you, showing you." His voice lowered, thickening with the depth of his emotions. "Oh, sweetheart, you don't know how I've dreamed of you. There were times I actually felt you next to me; I could smell your perfume, taste you on my tongue. And when I woke up and you weren't there, I cursed my own stupidity. You were always with me, just out of reach in my dreams."

Blair blinked back tears. "Oh, Cameron." How many times had she experienced that same frustrating dream?

"But I don't want you in my dreams," he continued huskily. "I want to be in *our* bed, with you naked in my arms. I want to run my hands over your breasts, your thighs. I want to kiss every inch of your gorgeous body until you beg me to take you. Does that," he growled, "satisfy your curiosity?"

"Yes," she whispered. His words slid over her, wrapping a sensual spell around her. Her imagination overruled her more sensible instincts and placed his hands and mouth on all the secret yearning places of her body, and she wished desperately that he was there with her, holding her close to his hard male being, loving away the hurt of the past, the insecurities of the future, so that there was only room for the present, for him, in her thoughts.

"Why don't you let me come over and show you how I feel?"

Her eyes flew open. "No!" She jerked into a sitting position and flipped on the bedside light, her heart racing with sudden panic and yes, excitement. The urge to say yes was so strong, she had to bite her lip to hold the word back. She knew herself too well. Once she gave in to him, she would be lost. The problems between them would be buried by an avalanche of desire that would obliterate everything. Only later would their differences rise to haunt them. "No, Cameron, not tonight."

"When, then?" he demanded.

"I don't know. It's late and I'm too tired to discuss it. Can't we save this discussion for another time?"

"No, dammit, we can't!" His expletive more than adequately expressed his frustration. "I'm tired of you keeping me at arms' length, pretending that you don't feel the same way I do. We've got to talk this out, Blair."

She could feel her resistance weakening. "I know. But I don't want you to come over tonight."

"Honey, I'd never push you into something you're not ready for," he assured her. "But I can't let you run away from me forever."

"I'm not running," she protested weakly. "I'm trying not to make another mistake."

"*We* are not a mistake," he said swiftly. "We never were. If you'll just forget the past and remember the good times, you'll see I'm right. What time are you coming over Friday night?"

She frowned in confusion. "Friday night?"

"It's your night to cook," he reminded her dryly. "Why don't you come around seven? And do you think your mother or Caroline will look after Julie? We need this time to ourselves."

The underlying anxiousness of his words pulled at her heart, and she knew she couldn't deny him the response he wanted. "Would you like anything special for dinner?" she asked softly.

His laughter was warm and intimate, heady. "Yes, but that's a surprise. I know you'll be tired after working all day, so I'll buy the supplies myself. You just bring yourself and I promise it won't take you longer than two minutes to cook dinner."

"Two minutes!" she scoffed, smiling. "It can't be much of a meal."

"There was a time when you thought it was better than caviar."

"I don't like caviar."

"I know," he chuckled. "So I can't lose, right?" Before

she could say another word, he said huskily, "I'll see you Friday night, love. Don't be late."

The clock had never moved more slowly. For the next two days Blair watched it incessantly, cursing its slowness, burying herself in work as a welcome distraction. The nights were hardest. She lay in her big, empty bed and stared at the ceiling, picturing Cameron doing the same, wondering if he was counting the seconds as she was. She couldn't think of the future, couldn't think of anything except that, after all this time, she was finally going to be with him again; they would finally be able to break down the barriers between them. Their coming together, like the aging of fine wine, would be sweeter for the wait.

By late Friday afternoon she was a nervous bundle of anticipation. When her mother walked into her office with Julie, she gave them a tremulous smile. "I see you two are ready to go. Who are you shopping for?"

"You and Daddy," Julie said excitedly. "Grandma said you needed a ro—"

Margaret Johnson hastily muffled Julie's words with her hand, a rueful smile tugging at her mouth at the sight of her granddaughter's dancing eyes. "You're not supposed to tell Mama what you're getting her, Julie. It's a surprise."

Julie looked at her mother, her eyes big and round. "Oh. I forgot."

Blair grinned, her voice laced with tender laughter as she said, "That's all right, sweetheart. I didn't hear a word. Now, run and get your coat."

After Julie had left the room, her mother asked, "Would you like me to keep her all night? If you're going to be out late, that would probably be better anyway."

"Oh, Mother, would you?" Her mother was dying to know what was going on between her and Cameron. Blair could see it in her eyes. She bit back a smile and put her arm around Margaret's shoulders. "Cameron and I have some things to discuss, and I don't know how long it will take."

"Take your time, honey," Margaret Johnson said quickly.

"I'm not trying to put any pressure on you, but you know how I feel about you and Cameron getting back together. You two belong together."

"I know," Blair replied huskily. "It's taken me a while, but I know now that I still love him. I guess I always have."

After they had gone, Blair walked slowly upstairs, her eyes lit by a fire that had been deliberately extinguished since the day she walked out of the courthouse with her divorce papers in hand. She had convinced herself she couldn't love a man who had hurt her as Cameron had, and for two long years she had honestly believed that. She resolved to forget him and go on with her life, but somehow she never did, despite Caroline's constant attempts to push her out of the past. Now she could see that her heart had switched to automatic pilot and that she hadn't experienced one single honest emotion until Cameron had walked into Stan's party. She felt as if she were a butterfly emerging from a cocoon, confused, hesitant, but eager to fly.

When she knocked on Cameron's door promptly at seven, her heartbeat was so erratic that it shook her knees. She was breathless, giddy, practically singing inside, and one look at her and he would know she was ready to fall into his arms. Suddenly she laughed. Cameron wanted to talk, but would he still want to once he saw her dress, smelled her perfume? Wryly she admitted she may have gotten a little carried away. The cranberry silk of her dress swirled about her, the softly draped bodice sighing with her shallowest breath, the skirt hugging her hips enticingly before falling below her knees in gentle folds. Ah, well, she told herself. So she had put a touch of romance into her dress. That didn't mean . . .

The door opened with a jerk, catching her by surprise, catching the laughter in her eyes. But at the sight of Cameron standing in the doorway, a short terry robe wrapped around his lean form, water sparkling in the dark tangle of his uncombed hair, she gasped. She had seen him like that many times, but this time was just like the first time and left her just as dazed. She swallowed convulsively, her mature veneer of poise deserting her in a flash.

Cameron grinned, his eyes devouring her. "Come in, Blair. You caught me with my pants off."

"'... said the spider to the fly,'" she mumbled when she was at last able to find her voice.

He laughed and pulled her inside, his hands going to the buttons of her coat before she realized what he was doing.

She didn't even try to help him. The clean, slightly spicy scent of his just-washed body assailed her, assaulting her senses in billowing waves of masculinity and driving all coherent thought from her head. She closed her eyes weakly and felt his hands move lingeringly over the buttons. Over the top of her head he spoke, his warm breath stirring her hair. "Don't worry. I'm not going to accost you the minute you walk in the door. I'm just running a little behind schedule." He slid the coat from her shoulders, his eyes following the path of his hands, his mouth lifting in a dazzling smile as he inspected every inch of her. "Beautiful!" he said huskily under his breath. His fingers traced the outline of her lips. "Make yourself at home while I get dressed."

She watched him disappear down the short hallway that obviously led to the bedroom, quelling the urge to follow him. Shaking her head ruefully, she took several deep breaths and stepped into the living room. Cameron's personality was clearly reflected in the room. The furniture was large, comfortable, and mostly of leather, expensive but not ostentatious. An oak wall unit dominated one end of the room, economically holding an elaborate sound system, video recorder and portable television. Books lined the two adjacent walls and cluttered the coffee table and floor near the couch in a disarray she remembered well from the days of their marriage.

Almost blindly she walked away from that thought to stare unseeingly out the wide windows, which offered a breathtaking view of the bay. Instead she saw the vacant shelves that the removal of those very books had left in her own home. For months after the divorce those shelves had taunted her, their very emptiness symbolizing the echoing chambers of her lonely heart. She had intentionally avoided the study until, one ambitious weekend, she had filled every shelf with books, figurines, magazines—anything to distract her from the aching emptiness.

Cameron walked back into the room, his hair now neatly combed though still damp, a biscuit-colored silk shirt clinging to the wide breadth of his shoulders, beige slacks covering his slim hips. He immediately spied her by the windows and eliminated the distance between them in three long strides.

"Are you ready to start dinner?" he asked huskily, his eyes devouring her.

The dull thudding of her heart echoing in her ears, Blair struggled to find her voice. "Yes, of course."

"Good," he growled, reaching out to take her hand, his eyes soft and warm, incredibly tender, as they met hers. "Come on. I'll help you."

"Cameron..." she protested halfheartedly, unable to fight the pull he had on her hand, her heart, "I'm being paid to cook your dinner. You must let me do it."

The black depths of his eyes glowed with promise. "There's nothing in our agreement that says I can't help you, is there?"

"No, but—"

"No *but*'s." He laughed, pushing open the door to the kitchen. "Anyway, this is a special dinner, just for the two of us. It wouldn't be the same if I didn't help."

"What do you mean?" She frowned as the light in his eyes made her distinctly uneasy. "What are we having?"

"Chili dogs and Ripple Wine."

Memories hit her full in the face. The first night of their married life, they had driven to Cape Cod to take the ferry to Cameron's parents' beach house on Martha's Vineyard. She could still feel the cold wind swirling around them as they stood at the bow, wrapped in each other's arms. They were freezing but exhilarated when they finally reached the house, and Cameron had deliberately delayed the inevitable conclusion to the evening by cooking chili dogs and plying her with the inexpensive wine.

"Do you remember?" Cameron asked quietly, taking a step closer, his nearness scorching her like a furnace. "We

Made in Heaven 87

lay by the fire and drank wine from the bottle."

"And you got very warm, so I helped you off with your shirt...." Her voice was now a whisper, the memory of his firm chest under her fingertips creating an almost physical ache in the pit of her stomach.

"And I, of course, had to return the favor." He touched her cheek, wonderingly tracing the fiery color that sprang to life there. "I'm glad you haven't forgotten."

"How could I forget my own wedding night?" By the time they had moved on to the vast feather bed, the wine, the chili, and Cameron's nearness had stoked a furnace inside her that burned for the duration of the long, delicious night. "It was beautiful."

He smiled. "Yes, it was. And now that I know you're not going to kill me for reminding you of it, I can relax. And help you. Okay?"

"Okay." Tonight, she thought wryly, she probably wouldn't be able to deny him anything.

The kitchen was sparse, equipped with only the rudimentary tools needed for basic survival. Cameron had never been much of a cook. When he was caught up in his work, his fingers banging away at the typewriter, food was the last thing on his mind. He could subsist on peanut-butter-and-jelly sandwiches for days at a time. Judging from the spotlessness of his kitchen, he hadn't spent much time there since his return to Boston.

"Did Julie rebel at being left behind?" he asked as he took the wine and hot dogs from the refrigerator.

"No. She went Christmas-shopping with my mother." She opened several cabinet doors in a futile search for pots and pans. "Where's a pot for the chili?"

"In the cabinet to your right." He opened the wine and poured them each a glass. "To a happy reconciliation," he saluted her, his eyes challenging her to make the toast.

Blair lifted her glass and eyed it thoughtfully. "I have a feeling I shouldn't be toasting anything. I need to keep a clear head tonight."

"Believe me, sweetheart, it's not the wine that's going to cloud your brain."

When the food was ready, they sat across from each other, mesmerized, Cameron's hand straying toward hers, his knees brushing hers under the table, setting her nerves atingle. A flash of desire sparked and burned deep within her, growing stronger as each touch added kindling to the fire. In desperation she took a cooling swallow of wine and choked as its sweetness washed away the spicy taste of the food. "Ugh! That's awful together!"

Cameron laughed, his teeth flashing in a grin that went straight to her heart, his eyes sparkling with amused indulgence. "It's not a very good combination, is it?"

"That's putting it mildly," she chuckled, wrinkling her nose as she pushed her plate away. "Somehow I've lost my appetite."

"Good. Now we can get comfortable." He rose to his feet and pulled her up beside him, his hand settling on her waist, singeing her skin through the silk of her dress. Her pulses pounded, stealing her breath, and when he urged her back into the living room, she made no protest. She sank onto the thick cushions of the couch and watched him take a place beside her, not close but within touching distance. His eyes met hers over the rim of his glass. "Has there been anyone else, Blair?" he asked suddenly. "I wouldn't blame you...."

She set her glass down with fingers that had an unexpected urge to tremble. "You realize, I hope, that that's none of your business," she said tightly. "Just as it's none of my business what you've been doing for the last two years. I don't know what you've been doing, who you've been seeing, and I don't care to know."

"Liar," he growled, the wicked flash of his teeth mocking her indifference. "You're dying to know. Believe me, you have nothing to worry about. There's not a woman on earth who could make me forget you."

"I was never worried about other women," she replied pointedly. *"That* I think I could have handled."

He didn't pretend to misunderstand her. "You could have handled my devotion to work, too, if you hadn't been so young. You wouldn't have any problems with it now."

Made in Heaven

"My age had nothing to do with it." Her eyes met his earnestly, baring her feelings without a qualm. "You've always insisted on misunderstanding me. I *never* asked you to give up your work for me. I just needed to know that if I called you, you would come. But you didn't. I even had to inform you of my pregnancy over the phone. You were off in the jungle somewhere, covering another stupid war." She heard the hurt in her voice and tried valiantly for control. At last she said simply, "I know you had your own dreams, and I didn't want to stand in your way. I just didn't expect my own dreams to be shattered for the success of yours."

"And what if I said that success was empty without you by my side?" He set his glass next to hers on the coffee table. His penetrating eyes latched on to hers and would not allow her to break the connection by lowering her eyes. "I mean it, Blair. These last two years I've just been marking time, waiting for a chance to get back to you. I knew when I accepted the London job without consulting you that I was making a mistake, but I was too bullheaded to admit it. Believe me, I paid for that mistake."

They had both paid for it in time that could never be regained. She stood up on shaky legs and walked over to look blankly at the books lining one wall. "Why *did* you accept the London job? Without so much as telling me."

"I don't know. I guess I was trying to prove to myself that I didn't have to answer to anyone. After all, it was *my* career."

She winced. "Well, that certainly lets me know where I stood with you."

"It does nothing of the kind," he said angrily. "It was a stupid, immature thing to do, and it almost destroyed us. Surely you can see it was a mistake. And I'm sorry for it, Blair. But we belong together, darling, and nothing is ever going to change that."

She hugged herself to ward off the sudden chill that ran down her spine. "I won't marry you again," she said flatly. "I won't make the same mistake twice."

Instantly he was behind her, his hands settling on her shoulders to turn her to face him. "You're right. Any marriage between us now would probably be another disaster. We need time, time to learn to trust again and not have it blow up in our faces. And you don't trust me, Blair. You're expecting me to walk away again, and I'm not going to do it."

His hands kneaded her tense shoulders, incessantly routing all rationality, all thought. She wanted to rest her head against his chest, to feel his arms binding her to him for all time, but caution fought the sensual dream he was weaving with his hands and she couldn't yield. Not yet. "The giving can't be all one-sided, Cameron. You have to make a few concessions yourself."

"If you only knew how much I want to give you..." His fingers abandoned her shoulders to cup her face and lift it to his. He brushed her lips lightly with his own before stepping away from her. "Get your coat. I'm taking you home."

She blinked in confusion. "Home?"

"That's right." His tone would brook no argument. Within minutes he had her bundled in her coat and back in the car. When he drew up in front of the red-brick facade they had once called home, he whisked her out of the car, took the key from her trembling fingers, and unlocked the door. Once they were inside, he frowned at the darkness, which was eased only by the light she had left burning in the entrance hall. "What's going on? Surely your mother and Julie are back by now."

"Julie's spending the night at my parents," Blair said softly.

"Well, that's just great," he said in disgust. He glared at her in growing irritation. "Why didn't you tell me?"

"What difference does it make?" Her bewildered eyes roamed his face. "Julie loves staying with my parents."

"I'm sure she does. But your mother was supposed to be here when I brought you home."

Feeling as if she were a particularly dense child, she frowned. "Why?"

"Because, Miss Twenty Questions," he replied huskily, stalking toward her with slow, purposeful strides, "I could hardly carry you off to our bed with your mother here. You do still have it, don't you?"

"Have what?"

"Our bed."

"Yes, of course." He was within touching distance, and she was finding it increasingly difficult to think. She must have had more wine than she thought. She lifted her hands to his chest to push him away and found them lingering instead, loving the feel of his rippling muscles under the smoothness of his shirt. "You promised you wouldn't rush me," she reminded him.

"I know." His arms closed around her and drew her to his chest. "Why did I make such a stupid promise?" He groaned against the side of her neck. "You know I can't keep my hands off you."

His head lowered toward her, blocking out the world, and she made one last halfhearted attempt at sanity. "Cameron..."

"Just one kiss," he growled against her trembling lips.

"Just one," she agreed, but he didn't wait for her answer. His mouth settled over hers possessively, his tongue delicately tracing the outline of her lips, ignoring their parted breathlessness for agonizing moments and driving her out of her mind with longing. He played with her mouth, teasing her, sweeping his tongue over the edge of her teeth with darting forays before retreating again until she was groaning in frustration.

She arched into him, her hands gliding up his chest to tangle in his hair to draw him closer, and still he wouldn't deepen the kiss. Her blood rushed through her veins like quicksilver, and his hands, which ran over the curve of her hips, pressed her against him and ignited an ache in her that burned at the very center of her being. Her tongue imitated his, languorously adoring the masculine curve of his lips, touching his teeth with teasing delight. He groaned and deepened the kiss, sending her senses spiraling upward to the stars.

The kiss went on and on until Blair's knees buckled and she was clinging to him weakly. He broke off the kiss abruptly and brought his steadying hands up to her shoulders. "I've got to go, but I can't leave you. I know it's too soon—we haven't settled anything—and I wanted you to ache for me."

"I do." She looked straight into his passionate eyes, letting him see how much she loved him, how much she needed him. The time for pretense was gone, all thought of resistance—all thought of denying him the pleasure they could find in each other's bodies—incinerated on a rising flame of desire. She hugged him to her, her arms going around his broad shoulders, the curves of her body fitting naturally to his hard angles and planes. "Don't you know I've ached for you for two lonely years?" she whispered. "Let's go to bed, darling."

He needed no further encouragement. He swept her up against his chest and took the stairs in long, easy strides, his eyes searching out hers in the darkness. "Are you sure, Blair? I don't want any doubts between us."

How could she doubt something that was so right? She had waited what seemed like an eternity for him. Even had she had a flicker of doubt, she would have cast it away. This night was theirs! "The only thing between us right now"—she laughed softly as he carried her unerringly into her bedroom—"is too many clothes. Do you think you could get rid of some of them?"

"Oh, I'm sure of it." His fingers worked at the buttons of her coat and it dropped to the floor with a whisper. She shivered and his arms ran roughly up her arms, warming her. He leaned down to give her a swift, hard kiss. "Don't move," he said against her lips. "I'll light a fire."

He had already lit one in her, but she waited patiently, watching the strong, agile muscles of his back as he leaned over to set a match to the wood and kindling she always kept ready in the fireplace. She loved having a fire in her bedroom. There was nothing more romantic—and also nothing lonelier when there wasn't anyone to share it with. But he was there now and she wasn't going to worry for how long.

Flames leaped up, casting dancing shadows in the dark

corners of the room. Cameron took off his coat, stooped to pick up hers, and tossed them both to the wing chair by the fire. His smile flashed in the darkness, the muted light from the fire turning his eyes into shiny black orbs. He reached for her. "Now, where were we?" he murmured.

"You were about to seduce me," she teased, her hands plucking at the buttons of his shirt until they gave way to her inquisitive fingers. "And I thought you were going to get rid of some of these clothes."

He stilled her fingers. "This is a joint effort. Shall we see who can seduce whom?"

She read the challenge in his eyes and grinned. "You're on."

She hooked one hand around the strong column of his neck and brought his head down to hers to plant tiny kisses over every seductive curve of his mouth. Her hand moved fleetingly over the hard muscles of his chest, exploring familiar, dearly loved places before sliding around to his back and pulling his shirt free of his pants. Running her fingers down the column of his spine, she slipped them in the waistband of his pants and laughed softly when he groaned in response. "How am I doing?" she asked against his mouth, exhilarated with the power she had over him.

"Not bad. But let me show you how it's done." His fingers tunneled through her hair to hold her head still, and his mouth settled over hers to stop the butterfly kisses she had tortured him with. The gentle flick of his tongue coaxed her lips apart, taking possession of her with a single-mindedness that shattered her thoughts of teasing him and left her trembling in his arms.

The hunger in her spread from deep within her in wave after wave of need, coursing through her until every nerve ending in her body cried out for fulfillment. She shook with desire, with a passion that had lain dormant for two long, empty years. Hardly aware of the fact that he had unzipped her dress and pulled it and her bra from her, she slipped his shirt off with shaking fingers and gasped when his mouth and hands began their journey over her breasts with a languid slowness that was devastatingly effective. His lips lavishly cherished the taut crest of first one breast and then the other until she throbbed from his sensuous torture. When she was past thought, whimpering with her need for him, his arms welded her to his body from hip to chest, and his mouth returned to hers in a deep driving kiss that blocked out everything but the two of them.

Blair arched into him, pressing her swelling breasts against his hair-roughened chest, entreating him to come to her. Her fingers went to the clasp of his slacks, unfastening it, copying his own skillful removal of her clothes. At last they were naked, skin touching skin, the firelight creating enticing shadows on their bodies.

Cameron swept back the covers of the bed, lifted her into its soft middle, and followed her down. His eyes met hers in the dim light. "I've dreamed of holding you like this—kissing you until you were out of your mind with wanting me—and that's exactly what I'm going to do." His teeth nibbled at her sensitive earlobe, the tender skin between her breasts, the softness of an inner thigh. His caressing hands and lips gave no more than she was willing to give, asked no more than she asked of him. Together they built up the fires of their passion, each kiss, each touch, shared, adding more fuel to the flames. They drove each other to heights they only dimly remembered but longed to return to, and only when her breathless sighs mingled with his muffled moans did he take them both into the exquisite realm that was composed solely of each other. Blair held him tightly to her, her eyes full of unsuppressed joy when they both floated back to earth in a lazy cloud of satisfied contentment. Cameron rolled away and brought her with him, his hand tenderly brushing back damp tendrils of hair from her face.

She snuggled against him, the fire that had consumed them still glowing in her green eyes. "Well?"

A dark brow lifted inquiringly. "Well what?"

"Who seduced whom the best?"

His mouth twisted into a smile as his arms tightened around her. "I think it was a draw. Shall we try for best out of three?"

They loved each other long into the night until they were both sated and exhausted. When Blair finally fell asleep, it was with her cheek against his chest, his arms around her, binding her to him even in sleep.

Sunlight streamed through the open curtains to dance on her closed eyelids. She groaned and reached for Cameron, only to have her hand touch the cold sheet. She sprang up in alarm, her body protesting at her sudden movement, her eyes alighting on the two coats draped over the wing chair. She sighed in relief and went to the closet for the comforting warmth of her old chenille robe. He was still there. For one terrible moment she had been afraid that last night had been nothing but a wonderful dream.

She tightened the sash of her robe and was looking for her house shoes when the bedroom door flew open and crashed heavily against the wall. Blair jerked around, her eyes widening at the sight of Cameron's thunderous expression. "Cameron! What's the matter?"

"Why don't *you* tell *me*?" he said softly, threateningly. He strode across the room and tossed a dozen red roses at her. "These just came for you. Along with this morning's paper."

Blair was too stunned to catch the flowers, and when the small white card and newspaper landed on top of them, she automatically reached for them, too. As soon as she lifted the paper, it fell open to the front page. In one stroke the headlines drove the blood from her cheeks and unhinged her knees. She collapsed on the edge of the bed. CONSTRUCTION GIANTS RIG BIDS. The words blinked up at her like a neon sign. She looked up in confusion. "What . . . ?"

He gestured to the card, which was lying in her lap. "Read it," he instructed coldly.

With shaking fingers she extracted the stiff piece of paper and stared blankly at the words scrawled in Stan's familiar handwriting. *A good newspaper man never ignores a tip. Sorry.*

Bid-rigging? A tip? Realization slapped her. Oh, no! She groaned, remembering what she had inadvertently told Stan about the incident at Kenneth Clawson's. But she hadn't told him anything concrete. How had he...? Damn him! He had no right to use whatever information he had gleaned from her careless remarks for his own gain. How could he do that? It could ruin her!

"Boy, you really played me for a fool." Cameron's mocking words brought her head up with a snap. "And I helped you every step of the way."

"Wh-what are you talking about?" she stammered, her heart suddenly squeezed by an awful foreboding. He was hurt—she could see the pain in his eyes—and she ached to comfort him, to kiss it and make things better, but he was like a wounded animal striking out at her.

"I think it's fairly obvious, don't you? You helped Stan scoop the *Gazette*." He stepped away from her, the wall that was suddenly between them almost physical. "Where did you get your information? From a client?" At her startled look, his brows drew together in a fierce frown. "That's what you did, didn't you? You relayed information about a client to a reporter. How could you do that?" he thundered.

"It wasn't like that." Her eyes pleaded with him to understand. "I was worried about something I had overheard, and I needed some advice. I was talking to Stan on the phone and it just slipped out."

"How convenient." He whirled away from her as if he couldn't stand the sight of her. Stiff and unyielding, he stared out the window. "I guess you weren't kidding when you said Stan was a special client. I just didn't realize how special. What else have you been doing for him? Did you run to him every time I told you my plans for the *Gazette?*"

His words slashed at her, making a mockery of the night they had just spent together, cutting her heart into pieces. Tears pricked at her eyes, but she ruthlessly pushed them back. She would not let him ruin everything now. Suddenly furious with herself for sitting there like a helpless female, she threw the newspaper on the bed, stomped over to his stiff form, and planted herself firmly in front of him.

"Did it ever occur to you that you may be jumping to the wrong conclusion about this?" she demanded, glaring at him. "That Stan may have taken unfair advantage of something I told him in confidence? But you don't want to hear that. You've got it all worked out in your head, and nothing I can say will change the answers you've already come up with."

"That's right," he snapped. "Evidently the services you offer your clients are more varied than I thought. Spying for Stan, making love with me... there's no end to your talents. And I was stupid enough to think that no matter what had happened in the past, you would still be loyal to me—to us. God, what an idiot I've been!"

Her hands reached out to him, his hurt bringing tears to her eyes as nothing else could. "Cameron, don't do this! You've got it all wrong."

He shook off her restraining hand. "Not any more, I don't." Pained disillusion clouded his eyes as they raked over her, the grim lines in his face suddenly making him look tired and defeated. "You're not the woman I thought you were. The woman I married, the woman I once loved, had too much integrity to betray a client's trust, let alone a husband's!"

"I didn't betray anyone," she cried in frustration. "And you're not..."

Ignoring her, he picked up Stan's card and thrust it under her nose. "It's right here in black and white, Blair. Every construction firm in the city is being investigated by the attorney general's office because of a tip you gave Stan. You can't deny that. And you can't deny that you took advantage of a privileged position to help Stan. Can you?"

Helplessly she stared at him. "Of course I can," she stormed. "In fact..."

"I think there's nothing more to say." Without another word he turned and walked out, impervious to the anguished tears that streamed down her face.

- 6 -

THE DOOR CLOSED quietly behind his retreating back, the coldness of his leave-taking utterly devastating to her. Blair felt as if she'd been turned to stone. Her face was ashen, and a sickening horror rooted her to the floor. Last night he had taken her to paradise and held the world at bay with the touch of his hands on her body, his kiss on her lips. Yet, with the arrival of daylight, the wonder of the night gave way to a reality that was all too brutal. God, what had happened?

She dropped to the bed, suddenly too weary to stand, causing the note from Stan to fall to the floor. Cursing softly, she snatched it up and crumpled it in a ball, wishing that Stan was there so she could throw it in his face. Did he have any idea what he had done to her?

Tears burned her eyes, searing her heart, but she blinked them back furiously. She would not cry! Damn Cameron! A rising surge of indignation carried her to her feet, and she paced restlessly, sparks of outrage flaring in her eyes.

How dare he question her integrity! Did he actually think she would make love with him at the same time she was conspiring with Stan to drive him to bankruptcy?

She stormed into the bathroom and fed her fury under the stinging spray of a hot shower. The water coursed over her chilled skin, warming her blood, and she pictured herself giving Cameron a taste of his own medicine. She soaped herself slowly, remembering all too vividly the feel of Cameron's hard, muscular body beneath her hands as she broke down his self-control with the knowing touch of her fingers, drove him out of his mind with long, drugging kisses that promised him everything. When she had him where she wanted him, she'd remind him that Stan would appreciate any information she could forward to him.

She smiled softly at the picture her imagination painted, and felt her body respond to the sensual machinations. She groaned and reached for the hot-water handle: The shower spray had gotten too hot. Dear Lord, what was she doing to herself?

With shaking hands she grabbed a towel and rubbed it briskly over her wet body, wiping out the shadows that beckoned to her. She pulled on a nubby green sweater that brought out the emerald of her eyes, and slipped into faded jeans, her furious thoughts arguing among themselves. Why did she let Cameron hurt her this way? She should have shown him the door the minute he started throwing accusations at her. But she loved him, even though she felt like he'd stabbed her in the heart. He didn't mean it. He *couldn't* mean it. He'd been hurt, striking out at her because he thought she had helped Stan. He had to come back and give her a chance to explain. But would he?

She shied away from the feeling of loneliness that that thought evoked. He would come back, and in the meantime she was going to get a few things straight with Stan. She shrugged on her coat and headed out the door.

Her eyes were alight with banked fires when she arrived at Stan's apartment a few minutes later. She found him nursing a cup of coffee, a blue terry-cloth robe haphazardly covering his lanky form. His hair was standing on end; his face unshaven and pallid. When the chair she jerked out from the kitchen table scraped against the floor in protest, he winced and looked at her reproachfully. "Must you be so loud so early in the morning?"

"It's almost eleven o'clock," she said dryly. "That hardly classifies as 'early.' What did you do, celebrate till the morning's edition hit the streets?"

"Something like that." He groaned and held his head in his hands. "God, I wish I were dead!"

"That can be arranged," she replied sweetly, without an ounce of pity. "In fact, I could wring your neck myself."

"What did I do?" he asked in bewilderment. "I haven't seen you since the party."

Just as Cameron had done earlier, she tossed the morning paper and the incriminating envelope on the table in front of him. *"This* is what you did. Do you have any idea who accepted the roses for me this morning *and* read the card?"

He grimaced. "Don't tell me..."

"You guessed it. Cameron." She got up and poured herself a cup of coffee, anger rattling her voice and the cup. "Damn you, Stan Harper! It would serve you right if I never spoke to you again. First you trick me into confiding in you, and then you break your promise not to use the information. Can't I even trust you to keep your word?"

"Now, wait a minute," he began indignantly, then winced and rubbed his temples. "I didn't use any information you gave me."

"Then why did you send me flowers?" she asked shrewdly. "You can't worm your way out of this, Stan. You incriminated yourself with the card."

"The flowers were my way of thanking you for pointing me in the right direction, that's all. You didn't give me any concrete information, so don't try to take credit for my scoop. I worked my tail off to get this story."

"I'm not taking credit for anything, dammit!" An unexpected lump in her throat thickened her voice. "You used me. I couldn't believe it when I saw the paper. You practically promised me you'd forget what I said, but I'm sure that the minute you hung up the phone you started digging into this. Didn't you?"

Guilt stained his cheeks. "All right," he said gruffly. "I was wrong to let you think I wouldn't follow up on the story. But I couldn't ignore it, Blair. Competition is fierce right now, and when I see a chance to beat the *Gazette*, I'm going to take it. I couldn't turn my back on this just because you were the one who gave me the tip. The law is being broken, Blair. Don't you think these men should be exposed for what they're doing?"

"That's not the issue." Her eyes locked with his. "Are you my friend or are you a reporter? If you're going to take notes on our conversations, I won't even talk to you."

"I'm sorry. I knew you were going to rake me over the coals for this, but I had to follow up on it." Impatiently he swept his fingers through his hair. "Can't you understand, Blair? This has nothing to do with friendship. This story offered a real opportunity in a tough time, and I couldn't pass it up. I was wrong, though, to trick you into giving me the tip. It won't happen again. I promise."

"I should have never opened my big mouth," she said dully. "I guess I just wasn't thinking clearly. And now Cameron thinks I accepted him as a client so I could spy for you." She pushed her coffee away, a bitter taste on her tongue. "He's told me some of his plans for the *Gazette*, and now he thinks I'll pass them on."

Stan swore softly. "How can he be so stupid? Any idiot can see you're in love with him. You always have been."

"Is that so obvious?"

"It is to me. So what are you going to do? At this point, talking won't do much good."

"I know," she replied gloomily. "Maybe I'll kidnap him and beat some sense into him."

But when she returned home, she was the one who felt as though she'd been beaten. The anger she had used to shore up her badly sagging confidence faltered and finally disappeared altogether, leaving her an aching mass of hurt. Her heart was bruised and torn, her spirit utterly defeated. The pain she had experienced over the divorce was only a twinge compared to what she was feeling now. It devastated her, sapping her strength and leaving her empty. She longed to throw herself on her bed and indulge in a fit of weeping that would make her forget everything. But she wouldn't. She'd be damned if she'd let Cameron destroy her a second time!

Clamping her jaw in an angry line, she spent the next three hours exhausting herself by cleaning the house. In her present mood, no chore was too tedious as long as it kept her busy and filled the time. When her mother and Julie came in, they discovered her upstairs, polishing the walnut wainscoting of the hallway that ran the length of the house. Blair immediately plastered on a bright smile that she hoped would fool her mother and wrapped her arms a little desperately around Julie's small form. "Hi, sweetheart. I was wondering when you'd come home. Did you have a good time?"

"Oh, yes!" Julie grabbed her hand and pulled her toward the stairs. "Come and look at the presents, Mama. Is Santa coming tonight? You said he'd come soon."

"Three more days," Blair replied, laughing, as she allowed the child to lead her downstairs. "He'll be here before you know it." At the sight of the two large boxes under the tree, Blair shook hers and made outrageous guesses as to its contents, but when Julie finally went upstairs to play, Blair could see the suspicion in her mother's eyes. She rushed to avert it. "I've still got a million things to do, and I don't know how I'm going to get it all done before Christmas. I've finished shopping for gifts, but I haven't bought any food for the party or Christmas dinner. I did get the house cleaned, so at least that's out of the way."

"What's the matter, Blair?" Margaret Johnson asked, her eyes troubled. "Is there something wrong?"

"No, of course not," she replied, a little too quickly. "I've just been pushing myself lately. I'll be glad when

Christmas is over and everything gets back to normal." She looked at her mother glumly. Would life ever be normal again?

"How did last night go? Did you and Cameron come to an understanding?"

Hysterical laughter threatened to choke her. Cameron had reached an understanding without any help from her. "It was fine," she lied. "We had a long talk and then he brought me home."

Her mother remained unconvinced. She frowned, her searching eyes inspecting Blair closely. "Are you sure? You look a little down, and you weren't that way yesterday when I picked up Julie."

"I'm just tired," Blair assured her. "I've been thinking of taking a vacation after the Christmas rush—maybe get away from the cold and relax in the sun somewhere. What do you think?"

"I think that's an excellent idea."

They were soon discussing the different winter vacation spots, and Blair heaved a sigh of relief. She successfully distracted her mother for the next half hour, and when Margaret finally left, Blair was convinced she had put her mother's fears to rest. If only she could convince her own heart so easily.

The shadows of despair swirled around her, threatening to drag her down to the pits of self-pity. She stiffened and hurried upstairs to her room. The packages she had spent the better part of the week buying had piled up, and she knew it would take hours to wrap them all. She grabbed scissors, tape, and wrapping paper and thanked God for the distraction of work.

Minutes or possibly hours later Julie stood on the threshold. "What are you doing, Mama?"

Blair swept her hair back from her eyes and grinned tiredly. "I'm trying to wrap these presents. Why don't you come in and help me?"

That was all the encouragement Julie needed. Blair assigned her the task of picking out the wrapping paper for each gift and patiently listened to her recital of all she had done with Grandma and Grandpa. For the first time that day Blair began to relax.

"Look, Mama," said Julie presently, grinning as she held up a box she had decided to wrap. "Isn't it pretty?"

The wrapping paper could hardly be seen for all the tape that covered it, and Blair couldn't help but laugh as she took the package. "Yes, sweetheart, it's beautiful. Next time, though, let's not use quite so much tape."

"Okay," Julie said brightly, her dimples flashing as she reached for an expensive brown leather wallet. Her eyes, so like Cameron's, sparkled with interest. "Is this Daddy's?"

"No."

"Where's Daddy's present?"

Blair winced. She had bought Cameron a gift, but now she doubted whether she would ever give it to him—not after that morning. He wouldn't want anything from her, least of all a silver tie clasp in the shape of an old-fashioned feather quill pen. The symbol of a scribe would only remind him of her supposed treachery with Stan. "I might have to take Daddy's present back. I don't think he'll like it." Before Julie could ask any more questions, Blair added: "And why don't you start taking some of these down for me? I'll go cook dinner."

In the kitchen she practically threw frozen fish sticks and french fries into the microwave. Tonight was not the night for cooking anything complicated.

She set the table with controlled force. Christmas was only three days away, and she'd never felt less like celebrating. The sound of Christmas music from a TV special floated into the room, and she grimaced, fighting the hollow feeling that threatened to overtake her. In desperation she called out in a voice that was not quite steady, "Turn off the TV and wash your hands, Julie. It's time to eat." The music continued and she frowned in annoyance. "Did you hear me, Julie? Turn off the TV."

"She heard you, but I told her to keep it on. I want to talk to you." Cameron stepped through the swinging door, his expression grim, his eyes determined.

She felt as if she'd been kicked in the stomach. In the

small confines of the kitchen, his presence overwhelmed her and flashing images of the past whirled before her dazed eyes. In self-defense she turned her back on him, on the memories, and tried to ignore her shaking knees and shortness of breath. Her only coherent thought was to act as if she couldn't care less that he had once again turned her life upside down. Her voice betrayed her, however, when she choked out, "How did you get in?"

"Julie answered the door," he replied quietly. "I have something for you. If you'll turn around, I'll give it to you."

She took the food out of the microwave and almost dropped it at his words. He had given her so much already—heartache, loneliness, pain. She couldn't take any more. "After what happened this morning, I can't believe you'd want to give me anything."

"Dammit, Blair will you turn around?"

She couldn't. If she did, she was sure she'd end up in his arms, bawling like a baby. Instead she carefully set down the dish that held Julie's supper and grasped the edge of the counter, not even noticing that her knuckles were turning white. "No. I want you to leave. I'm too upset by what's happened. Let me and Julie get on with our lives."

"I can't," he said simply, coming up behind her on silent footsteps, his warm breath caressing her nape, tickling her senses. He thrust his arm around her and held a bouquet of yellow and white daisy mums in front of her face. "I'm sorry."

She stared blankly at the flowers, unable to get a word past the lump in her throat. Her favorite flowers. Would she ever be able to look at them again without remembering this moment? She buried her face in them and quipped, "Flowers twice in one day. This must be my lucky day. Do these have a card, too?"

"They don't need one. I've spent half the afternoon composing an apology," he admitted huskily. "I know it by heart. Would you like to hear it?"

"Listening to you is what got me into this mess," she said bitterly. "I've heard just about all I want to hear."

Tenderly he reached up to brush at the tawny strands of

Made in Heaven   107

her hair. "You don't want to hear that I've cursed myself a thousand times for doubting you? Hurting you? As soon as I walked out this morning, I knew I had just made the biggest mistake of my life. And I was scared, sweetheart, so scared that I had completely destroyed what we'd had over the last few weeks—what we had last night."

His deep voice wrapped around her until warm, sweet honey flowed through her veins, melting her, turning her to putty. But she couldn't lean back against him; her injured pride wouldn't allow it. And words, after all, were his business. "This isn't going to work, Cameron."

His arms slid around her, his hands settled on her waist. He pulled her back against him, inhaling the fragrance of her hair. "What do you want from me?" he murmured. "Ask and it's yours. I'll even get down on my knees for you if it'll melt your heart."

Panic seized her when he moved away from her. "No!" she cried, whirling to grab his arm and stop him before he even bent a leg. "I...I don't want you on your knees." Suddenly terrified of the crumbling walls of her control, she stepped hastily to the kitchen door. "Come and eat, Julie. Your food's getting cold."

Julie ran into the room, her expectant gaze going from Blair to Cameron. Finally she said, "Is Mama still mad, Daddy?"

"Yes, I think she is," Cameron replied quietly.

"Didn't she like her flowers?"

"I don't know." He studied Blair thoughtfully before turning to Julie. "Mama and I will be in the living room, sweetheart. You go ahead and eat."

Blair opened her mouth to protest, then abruptly shut it. She'd seen Cameron before with that determined glint in his eyes, and it was useless to argue. Stiffly she handed Julie her supper, then preceded Cameron into the living room, waiting for the kitchen door to swing shut before turning to face him. "All right," she said over the pounding of her heart, "I'm listening."

Cameron reached over to turn off the TV. "Are you going to accept my apology or not?"

"Give me one good reason why I should," she challenged.

"Because I behaved horribly," he replied promptly, catching her off guard. "When I saw the headlines, I wanted to rake a few butts over the coals for letting that story get past us. When the flowers and card arrived from Stan, I saw red and took out my frustrations on you."

"That doesn't excuse you," she said quietly, hurt tightening her throat. "You actually thought I would spy on my clients, on you—"

"No, honey, I didn't. That was just anger talking. The minute the words were out of my mouth I wanted to kick myself. You've got to believe that."

She searched his face, her eyes tortured as she admitted, "I don't know what to believe. You said we needed time to trust each other. But if this morning is an example of your kind of trust, I don't want it."

"Blair, honey, don't do this to us." He moved toward her, his hands reaching for her and closing over her shoulders. "Don't let this come between us," he whispered. "I take full responsibility for this morning, and I promise you it won't happen again. Last night—what we shared—was too important to be overshadowed by my stupidity this morning. You could have never given yourself to me the way you did last night unless you loved me. *That's* what counts. Let's just forget the rest."

Tears burned her eyes. "I could have killed Stan when I found out he used me...."

"Shh," he said softly, his fingers pressed against her lips to still her words. "It's not important. You're all that matters to me. Please say you forgive me, sweetheart."

At the look in his eyes Blair felt the bottom drop out of her world, leaving Cameron to cling to. She staggered under the onrush of desire that swept over her, battering her resistance, beckoning her to its sweet ecstasy. She wavered, torn by conflicting emotions, but when Cameron leaned down to kiss her, a relieved gleam in his eyes, she rebelled. "No!"

Catching him by surprise, she wriggled free of his hold

and put half the distance of the room between them before he realized what had happened. Confusion flickered in his eyes. "What do you mean, no? No, you don't forgive me?"

"No, I don't want you to kiss me," she exclaimed breathlessly, her heart catching painfully when the anxiousness in his eyes turned to disappointment. He took a step toward her, determination apparent in the set of his jaw, and she hurriedly put the couch between them. "I'm not playing games," she warned him, "so if you really want me to forgive you, you'd better think twice before you take another step."

That brought him up short. "Of course I want you to forgive me. I thought I had convinced you of that."

"Then give me some time." Her eyes bared her pain, letting him see just how much she was hurting. "I couldn't take another morning like this morning, Cameron. I can't take any more hurt."

He made a motion as if to step around the couch and she backed up warily. He cursed softly. "Honey, if you'd just let me touch you, hold you."

"No!" she choked out in panic. "I won't let you sweep me off to bed every time you want to win an argument. We'd spend all our time in bed and you'd win all the arguments."

His mouth lifted in a wry grin, unexpected amusement shining in his eyes. "You must admit, that's an interesting proposition. Are you sure you don't want to try it out?"

"I'm positive. You know I can't think when you're close to me."

He smiled tenderly. "You do the same thing to me, sweetheart. Who needs to think? Just do what comes naturally."

"I did, and look what happened this morning." Cursing the hurt ring of her voice, she strove for a calmness she was far from feeling. "I mean it, Cameron. Last night was a mistake. Surely after this morning's fiasco you can see we're not ready for a physical relationship." When he didn't answer, she gritted her teeth in frustration. She was wasting her breath. He was just waiting for the chance to step around the couch and sweep aside her objections. And he could do it, too. One touch and she'd be lost. She had to convince him. "We either do things my way or you can forget it. Take your choice."

They measured each other shrewdly, the threat hanging between them, tension ticking away like a time bomb. Just when she thought she couldn't bear the silence another second, he said gruffly, "You're right. I hurt you and that's the last thing I wanted to do. So no sex. For now. But I reserve the right to try and change your mind."

"You can try, but you'll be wasting your time," she said with false bravado. She still stood with the couch between them, unable to believe that he was giving in so easily.

"Maybe. Maybe not." He sat down on the couch and patted the space next to him. "Now that we've got that straightened out, come and sit next to me so we can talk."

She shook her head and walked toward the kitchen. "I've got to check on Julie and clean up the kitchen. If you want to talk, you'll have to do it in there."

He caught up with her easily, his voice mocking as he murmured, "There's no point in running, sweetheart. You can't run from your feelings."

She tried to ignore the accelerated beating of her heart and desperately wished he wouldn't stand quite so close. His warm breath fanned her neck and sent out sensuous signals she was powerless to ignore. She quickened her pace and stepped into the kitchen two steps ahead of him. Julie was just getting up from the table, and Blair quickly dampened a paper towel and washed her hands and face before suggesting lightly, "Why don't you take Daddy upstairs and show him the puppy you want in the dog book I bought you last week."

Julie was halfway out of the room before she even finished speaking. "Come on, Daddy. Santa's bringing me a puppy. Don't you want to see what it looks like?"

"Of course I do." He grabbed her up in his arms and nuzzled her neck until she squealed in delight. His eyes met Blair's over the top of their daughter's head, silently telling her he knew exactly what she was up to, before he turned his attention back to Julie. "A puppy's a lot of work, you know. You have to feed him and take care of him. Do you think you can do that?"

She lifted her chin, unwittingly copying Blair. "I'm a big girl. I can do it."

Their voices faded as they made their way upstairs. The coldness of the morning was warmed by the gentle glow Blair had experienced at the sight of Cameron and Julie laughing together. They needed him and he needed them. The last two years had been empty without him, and the rest of her life would be just as empty if he wasn't part of her world. Somehow she had to make him understand that all she wanted in life was him by her side. And yet, her old reservations, her bitter hurt of that morning, wouldn't allow her to let down her defenses, to submit to him. . . .

She finished straightening the kitchen, and still Cameron and Julie had not come down. The living room was quiet, with only the fire crackling on the hearth. Blair sank down onto the couch, too tired to climb the stairs to see what Cameron and Julie were doing. The warmth from the fire weighted her eyelids, and she closed them with a sigh.

"Blair . . . sweetheart . . ."

"Hmm?" She frowned, Cameron's husky voice summoning her from the depths of sleep. She turned her head and nestled her cheek against the unyielding pillow that cushioned her head, stretching languidly, luxuriating in the warmth that surrounded her.

"Don't you think you ought to go upstairs and go to bed," he suggested in a low voice, his warm breath caressing her ear. "It's getting late. . . ."

Blair's eyes flew open and she found her head resting on his hard thigh, her eyes level with the zipper of his slacks. She blushed crimson and jerked to a sitting position, her composure shattered. With shaking hand she pushed her hair back from her face and tried to clear the confusion from her fuzzy brain. "How . . . ?"

"You fell asleep," he said softly, the hard lines of his face gentle with tenderness. "I came downstairs and found you all hunched over the arm of the couch. I couldn't leave you like that, and when I tried to make you more comfortable, it seemed only natural to use my thigh as a pillow."

Blair groaned. Even in her sleep she gravitated toward him! Fighting the blush that burned in her cheeks, she dragged her gaze away from his and looked around the room. "Where's Julie?"

"In bed. It's after ten o'clock."

"Ten o'clock! My God, why didn't you wake me?"

"You were tired. You didn't get much sleep last night. Besides," he added, "I like holding you while you sleep."

Her heart jerked in her breast. She scrambled off the couch and began folding the afghan he had covered her with. Her movements were as jerky as her voice. "You'd better leave now. The next three days are going to be pretty hectic, and I'll need all the sleep I can get."

He got to his feet and reached for the coverlet she held clutched to her breast like a shield. When he tugged on it, she stepped toward him, her expression wary. It didn't occur to her to let go of the afghan. He ran his finger across her lips. "What time shall I pick you and Julie up on Christmas Eve?"

"What?"

"Christmas Eve." He laughed, touching the tip of her nose teasingly. "Don't you remember? We always go to my parents' on Christmas Eve. Mother's really looking forward to it this year. It's been a while since we were all together."

A sickening feeling washed over Blair, and her eyes widened in distress. "Cameron, I'm sorry, but I can't go. I... I've made other plans."

He seemed to freeze, his eyes suddenly guarded. "What do you mean, you have other plans?" he demanded. "Our first Christmas together we agreed to spend Christmas Eve with my parents and Christmas Day with yours. We've always done it that way. How could you make other plans?"

His affronted tone was more than she could bear, and steam gathered within her. He had no right to take her for granted. "In case you've forgotten," she reminded him, "we aren't married. I don't answer to you anymore. I made plans for Christmas Eve long before you returned to Boston. I'm giving a party for my clients who don't have any family or can't go home for the holidays. Even if I wanted to—which I don't—I couldn't possibly back out at this late date."

He swore softly, his face reflecting his disbelief. "You're actually going to spend Christmas Eve with clients instead of your family?"

"I don't have much choice, do I?" The anger drained from her voice. "I don't suppose you'd want to come to my party instead of going to your parents?" When he only glared at her, she grimaced. "I didn't think so. Well, Julie was going to be with me, but if you want to take her with you, then I guess it'll be just me and my clients."

"Yes, I want Julie with me," he snapped. "I also want you, but I'm not going to change your mind, am I?"

"No."

He walked into the entrance hall and jerked on his coat, his movements stiff and irritable. When he turned to find her hovering in the doorway, his face was grim. "I'll pick Julie up at seven. Please have her ready." For the second time that day, he left the house in anger.

Blair dragged herself through the next three days with a determined smile on her lips. She knew Caroline could see through the lighthearted laughter, the forced holiday spirit, but she thankfully held her tongue. Blair had never been more miserable in her life. Cameron had been conspicuously absent. It brought home just how important he had become to her life. She missed him dreadfully.

Seven o'clock on Christmas Eve arrived much too quickly for Blair's peace of mind. Julie had been a bundle of energy all afternoon, and her own nerves were stretched taut, like rubber bands ready to snap. She dressed Julie much too early, then spent the next hour holding her breath, terrified that her daughter would spoil her clothes before she even left the house. When Blair went upstairs to dress, she settled Julie in front of the fireplace with a coloring book and made her promise not to move.

In her own room Blair pulled on a kelly green silk dress and smoothed it over her hips. The softly draped neckline nestled around the elegant lines of her throat and breasts without revealing anything. It was the dress of a seductress, its dark, simple lines hiding her body yet teasingly clinging to every feminine curve. The row of tiny covered buttons that traced her spine from neck to hip were designed to drive men wild. And she couldn't quite reach them.

She hurried downstairs and found her daughter busily scribbling in her coloring book. "Julie, can you button my dress for me, sweetheart? I can't reach the buttons."

"Oh, Mama, that's pretty!" Julie exclaimed, reaching out to feel the material. "Can I have a dress like that?"

She laughed. "When you're older, sweetie. Now, hurry up. Daddy will be here in a minute." She sat on the footstool so that Julie could reach the buttons, but she found it increasingly difficult to sit still. Julie wasn't having much success, and when the doorbell rang, hot color rushed into Blair's cheeks. Damn!

"I'll get it!" Before Blair could move, Julie raced to the door and threw it open. "Hi, Daddy!"

Blair got to her feet, achingly conscious of her dress gaping open at the back, and watched Cameron walk into the living room. He looked sinfully handsome in a tan corduroy jacket and matching pants, his white shirt open at the collar to reveal the strong lines of his neck. She watched his eyes soften as they focused on her, and knew that he was as strongly affected by her as she was by him.

"That's a beautiful dress, Blair," he said huskily.

Julie hopped on first one foot, then the other. "Mama can't reach the buttons," she supplied helpfully.

Cameron's eyes lingered on the bare shoulder that had slipped free. "I'll do those for you." Without waiting for her consent, he stepped behind her, his warm hands burning imprints into her back.

Blair swallowed and bowed her head so her hair wouldn't get in the way, praying he would hurry and end the subtle torture. But when he slipped the last button into place and kissed the back of her neck, he drove the breath from her body. His hands settled on her shoulders to turn her to face him. "Are you sure you don't want to change your mind? It's not too late, you know."

His soft cajolery tempted her oh, so sweetly. God, if he only knew how she longed to go with him! "Cameron, you know I can't."

His eyes told her that she could—just say the word and he would gladly handle everything for her. But she didn't, and his hands dropped away from her in defeat. He turned to Julie. "Kiss Mama good-bye, Julie. We have to go or we're going to be late."

Julie ran to give Blair a hurried kiss, her eyes following Cameron when he made a move toward the door. "Wait, Daddy. Don't go without me."

Despite her anxiousness to leave, Blair gave her a fierce hug. "Be a good girl. And remember, Santa's watching you."

"Will he come while I'm gone?" she asked as Cameron helped her with her coat. "I don't want to miss him."

"No, he'll wait till you're tucked into bed and fast asleep before he comes," Blair assured her. "Now hurry. Daddy's ready to go."

Cameron turned at the door to give Blair a reproachful glance that brought tears to her eyes. She looked away and winced when he shut the door quietly behind him. The strength seemed to go out of her legs and she collapsed on the first step of the stairs, loneliness engulfing her in its dark void. Her joy in the evening was gone, stolen by the dark-haired giant who had just left with her daughter and her heart.

- 7 -

FROM HER POSITION at the head of the table, Blair observed her dining room with all the objectivity of a stranger and could find no faults. Candles glowed warmly on the sideboard, the mirrored wall behind them projecting their dancing flames out into the room like sparklers. Poinsettias and more candles decorated the table, which was covered with mouth-watering dishes that were a dieter's nightmare. Roast duck with orange sauce, wild rice, green beans with hazelnuts, sautéed carrots—the food was as rich as the laughter and good cheer that surrounded them. Holiday spirits were high; no one seemed to mind the fact that the numbers were uneven, that there were two men for every woman. It was probably the most successful party she had ever given, and she'd never been more miserable in her life.

Depression pulled her spirits down to her toes. Oh, she said all the right things, laughed at all the jokes. Only she knew that her heart just wasn't in it. She tried not to think of Cameron's face when he had left without her, tried not to feel as if he had abandoned her. She was, after all, among friends.

Her heart, however, refused to cooperate. Christmas wasn't supposed to be like this. She wasn't supposed to be alone!

She knew she had no one to blame but herself, but that did little to alleviate the hollowness inside her that made her list like a ship gone aground. There was only one cure for the ache that consumed her, and he was out of reach. She sighed and flashed Tom Carlisle a smile that didn't quite reach her eyes. She had no recourse but to suffer through the evening as best she could.

She couldn't hold back a sigh of relief, though, when the party began to break up. She stood at the door and thanked her guests for coming, an added sparkle in her eyes now that the end was in sight. Only four revelers remained when Larry Walker stepped forward to envelop her in a bear hug that threatened to cut off her breath. She suffered the embrace good-naturedly but was totally unprepared for the second hug. She groaned laughingly and pushed at his chest. "Come on, Larry, you know the rules. Only one hug per customer."

"Where's your compassion, woman?" he teased, refusing to release her. "You're sending me out in this weather to a cold, lonely bed and you're begrudging me one extra hug? You're a hardhearted woman, Blair Wakefield."

"Don't give me that lonely-bachelor line," she chided him as she successfully extricated herself from his arms. "You're probably not even going home from here. And I know for a fact your bed isn't cold unless your electric blanket's out of commission."

He grinned, totally unrepentant. "Oh, Blair, what can I say? You know me too well." He leaned over and kissed her on the cheek. "Merry Christmas."

The door was pulled open to admit an icy blast just as Larry stepped back, and Blair found herself looking straight into Cameron's eyes. The cloud that had hung over her all evening lifted, and she forgot everything except that he was finally there. Her smile broke through and she stepped toward him. "Cameron..."

Julie danced beside him, struggling with a huge stuffed dog that was nearly as big as she was. "Look what Grandmother gave me," she exclaimed to Blair. "Isn't he pretty?"

Blair dragged her eyes away from Cameron and squatted down to bring herself to eye level with her daughter. "He's beautiful, sweetheart. Did Granddaddy give you that, too?"

Julie screwed up her face in puzzlement. "No, he gave me a piece of paper."

Blair frowned and looked at Cameron inquiringly. He laughed. "Stock in his company," he explained. "Every child should have a few shares."

Julie plucked at her sleeve to recapture her attention. "Daddy's spending the night. He's going to be here when Santa comes."

Blair froze, painfully aware of the fact that Julie's announcement had reached everyone in the entrance hall. A blush slowly burned its way up her neck and into her cheeks. She could have cheerfully sunk through the floor, but all she said was "Oh, really?" and rose to her feet in one graceful motion, her furious eyes telling Cameron that she definitely wanted to talk to him.

"I'll tell you about it in a minute," he said in a low voice, watching her warily. "Right now I think your guests are ready to leave, and I have to get a few things from the car."

"Can I be here when Santa comes, too?" Larry teased as soon as the door shut behind Cameron.

Blair grinned in spite of her best efforts to remain stern. She pushed him toward the door. "No, you can't. Don't you have somewhere to go?"

"Come on, Larry," Tom Carlisle chuckled. "Lay off. Can't you see the poor woman's dying of embarrassment?"

It was true, so there was no use denying it. She opened the door and pointed to the cold darkness just beyond the light that spilled out onto the steps and sidewalk from the house. "Out, gentlemen. The party's over." After much razzing and pretended outrage, they kissed her cheek and finally left.

When Cameron returned, loaded down with brightly wrapped packages, she was steaming and had to consciously quell the urge to trip him. Instead she followed him into the living room and watched in stony silence as he and Julie placed the presents under the tree. "You are not spending the night," she told his back flatly.

"But Daddy promised!" Julie wailed.

"That's right, sweetheart, I did," he assured her, looking over his shoulder at Blair. "You'd better go get ready for bed or Santa's going to fly over the house without stopping. Hurry, now. It's late." He watched her run to do as he said before turning his attention back to Blair. "We'll discuss this after Julie goes to bed."

Seething, Blair knew him well enough to know not to push the issue. Still, she found it increasingly difficult to hold her frustrations in check. Julie found a hundred excuses to delay going to bed, and Blair's nerves were ready to shatter by the time she located Julie's pajamas, gave her a drink of water, helped her set out milk and cookies for Santa, and kissed her good night. She came downstairs on shaky legs and went straight to the living room. She stopped short at the sight of Cameron sitting on the floor by the Christmas tree, a large cardboard box next to him. "What are you doing?" she demanded.

"What does it look like I'm doing?" He grinned broadly. "I'm setting up Julie's train."

For the first time she noted the sections of track laid out on the carpet before him. "You bought her a train?"

"No, I'm giving her mine. My mother packed it away years ago; it's probably a collector's item by now." He placed the track around the tree and grinned in satisfaction when he flipped the switch and the locomotive started chugging around the track. "Works like a charm. She'll love it."

Blair was sure she would, too, but she was in no mood to swallow her indignation. She frowned and moved farther into the room. "You're not spending the night, Cameron."

A dark eyebrow lifted mockingly as he grinned with apparent delight. "Oh? And who's going to throw me out?"

Blair ground her teeth in frustration. "Why are you doing

this? Just three days ago you agreed we weren't ready for a physical relationship. Are you going back on your word so soon?"

"No. I'm trying to salvage a merry Christmas for myself."

The quiet words held a wealth of meaning that tore at her heart. She stared at him. "What do you mean?"

"I mean I had a hell of an evening. I couldn't get my mind off you, and my father spent most of dinner pressuring me to give up this foolishness with the *Gazette* and come work for him." He got up and walked over to the fireplace to stare broodingly into the fire. "All I've been able to think about since I left here without you is that you should be by my side, preferably in my arms, but at least within touching distance. Don't ask me to leave, Blair. I won't. I'm going to spend Christmas with my wife and child."

It didn't occur to her to remind him of the divorce. They measured each other for long, tense moments before she said simply, "You can sleep in the guest room." Without another word she went into the kitchen and pulled a large box from the top shelf of the pantry. When she returned to the living room she looked down at the toys she had set aside to be put under the tree as presents from Santa, then looked up at Cameron. "Since you're the daddy, you get the job of assembling the toys. Mama gets to fill the stockings."

A slow smile broke over his face. "I should have known you had an ulterior reason for letting me stay."

"That's right. You've got to earn your keep."

As they worked, the silence that wrapped around them, binding them together, was comfortable and close, broken only by Cameron's occasional muffled curses. Blair finished filling the three stockings she had helped Julie hang before the child had trundled off to bed. She turned now as Cameron swore softly. "I can't understand why you're having such a hard time," she teased. "A doll buggy and cradle can't be that complicated."

"That's easy for you to say," he growled. "Why don't you try it if it's so easy?"

"Okay, I will." She sat down next to him and reached for the instructions. "You're just too impatient. You must admit, patience is not one of your strong points."

"You'd better remember that," he said softly.

With Cameron's eyes on her, his knee only a hairbreadth from hers, Blair found it incredibly difficult to concentrate, but she kept her eyes trained studiously on the paper in her hand. Her senses stirred at his nearness, yearning for a more intimate closeness. She tried to pretend he wasn't there, wasn't watching her, but it was an exercise in futility. In desperation she reached for the partially assembled buggy and snapped the seat section into place without realizing she had done it. "How did you do that?" Cameron demanded, leaning over to examine the toy carefully. "That's not how the instructions said to do it."

"Who reads the instructions?" she scoffed. "It's just common sense."

"Oh, really? And are you saying I don't have any common sense?"

She grinned brightly. "Well..."

Cameron groaned and stared at the ceiling. "How did I fall for a woman who has so little respect for my talents?"

"You couldn't help yourself," she replied pertly, rising to her feet. "Do you think you can finish the cradle while I run next door to Caroline's?"

"At this time of night? Whatever for?"

"They won't be asleep," she assured him. "Caroline's puppy-sitting for me."

"You bought Julie a puppy," he stated, his eyes suddenly gleaming devilishly.

She frowned, not liking the look in his eyes. "Of course I did. You know how much she wanted a dog."

"That's why I bought her one, too."

Blair sank to the couch. "You didn't!"

"Oh, yes I did." He grinned rakishly.

"What am I going to do with two puppies?"

"Buy a lot of dog food," he suggested.

"That's easy for you to say," she complained. "You're not the one who'll have to feed them and housebreak them.

Why didn't you tell me what you were planning to do?"

"Why didn't you tell me?" he countered. "You never said anything, so I just assumed you weren't getting her one. I didn't want her to wake up tomorrow morning and be disappointed."

"I don't think you have to worry about that," she retorted. "She'll be ecstatic, though..."

"She will." He got to his feet and patted her on the shoulder. "You're a good sport, Blair. And don't worry, you've got a few more hours before the hounds of the Baskervilles descend on you. In the meantime you can put the cradle together while I go next door for the puppy."

"But where's the puppy you bought? Don't you need to check on it?"

"No, Valerie's taking care of it tonight." He started toward the door. "I'll be right back."

The cradle proved a little more difficult than the buggy, but Blair had it assembled and placed in front of the tree well before Cameron returned. He must be talking to Mike, she thought as her eyes scanned the room. She realized with a start that this night would always be precious to her. During their marriage they'd never spent a Christmas Eve planning surprises for their daughter; she'd been too young. Would she have this one memory to haunt her every Christmas Eve for the rest of her life, or would there be many more, with Cameron always there to share the special magic of the night? If only she knew!

Cameron's return put an end to her musings. She flashed him a smile that in no way reflected her troubled thoughts. "Were they asleep?"

"Are you kidding?" he chuckled. "They opened their presents tonight, and it'll be hours before the kids can tear themselves away from their new video game."

When he set the box he was carrying near the tree, Blair leaned over to stroke softly the little bundle of fur, which was fast asleep. "I guess you'll be getting two new playmates tomorrow," she told the puppy. "I must be crazy!"

"No, just a pushover for kids and puppies," Cameron remarked, his eyes warm with indulgence as they rested on her. "If you plan to get any sleep tonight, you'd better hurry up and get to bed. Julie will probably be up at the crack of dawn."

"I know. For years I've waited for her to get old enough to enjoy Christmas, and now I think *I'm* too old." She picked up the cookies and milk. "How about a cookie, Santa?"

He took the plate of cookies but held the glass of milk up to Blair's mouth. "Drink up like a good little elf. You could use a few more inches."

"In height or width?" she teased before swallowing the contents of the glass under his watchful eyes. "I thought I was just right."

Cameron pulled her over to the mirror above the fireplace. "Actually," he said dryly, "I prefer my woman without a milk mustache." When she laughingly reached up to wipe it off, his hand stopped her. "I'll do it." Slowly, with infinite care, he leaned over and lazily licked the milk from her upper lip.

The intimate caress melted her insides to warm, golden honey. She was boneless, hypnotized by his nearness, high on his familiar scent. She lifted glowing eyes to his. "Am I your woman?" she whispered achingly.

"Of course," he replied just as ardently, his fingers tracing the curve of her cheek. "Was there ever any doubt of that?" His eyes caressed every inch of her face before coming to rest on her mouth.

"Are you going to give me a good-night kiss like you did your other clients?"

She studied him thoughtfully. "I don't think so."

A dark brow shot up in surprise. "Why not?"

"Because the last time you only wanted a kiss, it led to the bedroom. And we both know that was a mistake."

"And if I promised it wouldn't lead anywhere you didn't want?" he asked shrewdly. "What then?"

He was tempting her and they both knew it, but the urge to be back in his arms was too strong to resist. "Then I guess you'd get a kiss," she said lightly. *"But,"* she stressed when he reached for her, "you make sure you remember

I'm the one giving it."

"I'll remember," he assured her solemnly.

She placed her hands on his shoulders and stood on tiptoe to press a lingering kiss to his cheek. "There. Are you satisfied now?"

His eyes reproached her. "By no stretch of the imagination can that be called a kiss."

"You were always greedy," she said, laughing, as she put her arms around his neck to pull his head down to hers. "This time I'll give you a kiss that'll knock your socks off." She covered his mouth with hers, exhilaration coursing through her as her lips moved over his with lazy satisfaction, safe in the knowledge that he was letting her take control. It was a heady feeling. Her tongue slid along the masculine line of his mouth, urging an entrance that he willingly gave. She deepened the kiss with a growing insistence, allowing his arms and body to support her, loving the taste of him on her tongue.

Her heart was pounding in her breast, the blood rushing through her veins, when she reluctantly pulled her mouth free, but she couldn't stop herself from planting tiny, breathless kisses along his jaw. Cameron was keeping his word; he was following her lead. She lifted her head to look in his eyes and was lost in the desire reflected there. Willingly she pressed her hungry mouth to his.

Somewhere in that kiss, Cameron took the initiative, his mouth devouring hers, his hands knowingly exploring the curves of her body. She throbbed with her need for him, but when his knee nudged her legs apart and his hand slid down her stomach to the heart of her passion, her slumbering defense system screeched in alarm. She struggled up through her desire like a swimmer fighting for the surface. "No. No! You promised."

Cameron kissed the pounding pulse in her throat. "You don't really want me to keep that promise, do you sweetheart?"

"Yes, I do!" she cried, furious at the sudden tears that choked her. "You promised, and I'm holding you to it."

He groaned softly and released her. "I don't understand you anymore. The whole time we were married, you were unhappy because you wanted your husband with you at night. Well, here I am. What more do you want?"

"Yes, you're here now. But what if the *Gazette* doesn't make it? What if two months from now you get itchy feet and decide you don't want a desk job after all? I won't put Julie through another divorce, and I certainly won't put myself through one."

His smoldering eyes pierced hers. "When you said you wanted time, you weren't kidding. How long do you want? A month? Six months? Two years? Good Lord, Blair, be reasonable."

"I *am* being reasonable," she said stiffly, defensively. "But I can see there's no point arguing with you tonight. So I'm going to bed." She started toward the stairs.

"And how do you plan to get out of that dress?" he asked. "Or were you planning on sleeping in it?"

He was right, she thought angrily. Why did he always have to get in the last word? Somewhat huffily she presented her back. "Will you unbutton me?"

"What's the magic word?"

"Please," she said sweetly, hoping it would choke him.

If Cameron noticed the way that she leaned away from his touch, he ignored it. His fingers crawled down the buttons, seeming to luxuriate in the task, grabbing at her breath every time they slid lower. When the last button was reached, when she was holding her breath in a mixture of anticipation and anger at her ungovernable senses, he merely patted her on the behind and said, "Go to bed, sweetheart. You're worn out."

She was shaking in reaction by the time she reached the haven of her room, her control all but gone. She sucked in a ragged breath and sank into the armchair by the hearth, not even noticing that her dress had slipped down past her shoulders. She stared at the cold grate and saw the leaping fire in the living room, felt again the heat from Cameron's body.

With an agonized cry she jumped up and turned her back

on the memory, hastily stripping off her dress and jerking on her flannel nightgown. She crawled into bed, but her mind refused to let her escape so easily. She could smell Cameron's scent clinging to her skin and recall all too clearly his presence in her bed. She groaned and turned toward the wall. Sleep was a long time in coming.

It seemed as if she had barely closed her eyes when Julie jumped on the bed and peered intently at her in the darkness. "Mama? Are you awake?" she asked in a stage whisper.

Blair bit her lip to keep from smiling. "No."

"Daddy said I could get up if you were awake. Santa brought me a puppy!" she exclaimed excitedly. "And a doll and a buggy and—"

"And now you want to open your presents," Blair guessed with a chuckle, pulling her daughter into her arms to give her a hug and kiss. "I guess I can be persuaded to get up."

"That's good," Cameron said from the doorway, switching on the overhead light. "I was all too tempted to join you." He glanced at the cold hearth, then back at Blair's face. Blair could feel the blush staining her cheeks.

"Would you like me to light a fire?"

"No!" Cameron's crooked grin and dancing eyes were doing strange things to her heartbeat. He looked incredibly sexy in a navy velour shirt and gray slacks, his lean figure filling the doorway; and it took iron control for her to steady her voice and say calmly, "No, but you can light one in the living room. By the time you do that and put on a pot of coffee, I'll be dressed."

He nodded, although his eyes still searched her face questioningly. "All right. Julie, why don't you come with me, and you can turn on the Christmas-tree lights."

Blair took the time to steady her nerves and slow the pounding of her heart, but when she entered the living room a few minutes later, dressed in a blue plaid blouse and navy pants, she had no control over the sparkle in her eyes. A delighted grin spread across her face as she stepped into a chaos that showed signs of lasting all day. The train Cameron had set out the night before was running around the track, its engine spouting smoke and screeching a warning at every imaginary crossing. The puppies were yapping at the train, their excited barking spurring Julie's laughter as she joined the small furry animals in chasing the miniature train around the Christmas tree. Blair leaned against the doorjamb, chuckling.

Cameron moved to her side, holding out a cup of coffee. "Here. This will clear the sleep from your head."

She took one sip and nearly choked. "It will also put hair on my chest."

He laughed and took the cup. "Then I'd better take it back."

Drowning in the warm glow of his eyes, she reached out to touch his arm. "Cameron, about last night..."

"It's already forgotten." His arm encircled her waist and propelled her toward the Christmas tree. "I think we'd better open the presents before Julie dies of suspense."

Julie tore into her presents with gleeful abandon, and Blair found herself envying her daughter's uncomplicated acceptance of the practice of gift-giving. Julie didn't worry about the reasons behind a gift; she just gave and received with enthusiasm, no questions asked. She watched with barely suppressed excitement as Blair and Cameron opened their gifts from her. Blair exclaimed over the wine-colored velour robe, only to have the words die on her lips when Cameron held up the masculine counterpart. Her mother was up to her old tricks.

"See, Mama," Julie explained, "now you and Daddy match."

Blair avoided Cameron's dancing eyes and turned to her daughter. "Thank you, sweetheart. It's beautiful."

She grinned and looked expectantly from Blair to Cameron and back again. "Where's Daddy's present?"

Up until that moment Blair still hadn't decided whether to give Cameron the tie clasp. Now it seemed she had little choice. She reached under the tree and handed him the small package. "Merry Christmas, Cameron."

His fingers made short work of the wrapping paper, and when he lifted the lid and saw the feather quill clasp, his silence spoke louder than words. Blair felt her heart drop to her stomach and rushed to explain. "I wanted to get you something pertinent to your writing, but you don't really need anything. And then, when I saw this, I immediately thought of you and—"

He leaned over and cut off her words with his mouth, the passion of his kiss taking her by surprise. Blair found herself responding, needing to assure him that the gift had no negative connotations. She longed to give herself up to his kiss, to forget everything and just enjoy the moment for as long as it lasted, but the knowledge that Julie was watching them with great interest kept the kiss frustratingly short. She drew back first, her eyes warning him of Julie, but he ignored her silent message to sweep her back into his arms for a fierce hug. "Thank you, sweetheart."

"What did you get Mama, Daddy?" Julie asked, inching closer to them.

Cameron reached out to pull her close, his eyes crinkling with laughter as he grinned at his daughter. "Me."

Julie giggled, an arm around each of their necks. "That's silly, Daddy. How can *you* be a present?"

"It's easy," he replied, his eyes locking with Blair's. "I'm housebroken, I've had all my shots, and I'm loyal and loving. And I won't wander off and forget to come home."

"And he costs a fortune to feed," Blair told Julie, hoping Cameron wouldn't notice the slight huskiness of her voice. She jumped to her feet and grimaced at the disaster that had once been a neat, well-ordered living room. "I'll make a deal with you two," she said lightly. "If you'll clean up in here, I'll make chocolate-chip pancakes."

"All right!"

Margaret and Frank Johnson arrived soon after breakfast, their arrival creating laughter and excitement, especially for Julie, who was breathless at the sight of her new dollhouse. She was soon immersed in discovering all its secrets, and while Cameron helped Margaret Johnson with her coat, Blair grinned into her father's twinkling hazel eyes and enveloped his portly figure in a fierce hug. "Merry Christmas, Dad."

"Merry Christmas to you, too, honey," he replied, slipping his arm around her waist to keep her close for a moment. "I don't know if you know it or not," he teased, nodding at her mother, who was in the process of hugging Cameron, "but you've just made your mother's day."

Blair laughed, delighted with the world. "I know. Somehow I knew I would."

Cameron greeted her father with a handshake, genuine respect and affection lighting his face. "Frank, it's been a long time. How are you?"

"Just fine, son. It's good to see you here again." His approval was obvious, but no more than Blair had expected. Her father had always liked Cameron, appreciating the fact that Cameron solicited his opinion about business and respected the knowledge Frank had gained over the years as a C.P.A. for a medical supply company. They had a closer relationship than Cameron had with his own father, and Blair was relieved to see that the divorce hadn't changed that. They were soon discussing football and the upcoming bowl games.

Once they were alone in the kitchen, Margaret Johnson turned to Blair with sparkling eyes. "I'm so glad you two have finally worked things out! Anyone can see that you belong together. Julie's absolutely ecstatic and—"

"Nothing is settled, Mother," Blair warned her quickly. "So don't get your hopes too high. I'm taking one day at a time, so don't rush me."

"Oh, I would never do that. It's your decision, honey. I just want you to know that your father and I approve one hundred percent."

I know, I know, Blair thought with amusement, but she only said, "Thanks. I knew I could count on you and Dad."

Late that afternoon, after a delicious dinner that left everyone too lethargic to move, they relaxed in the living room, the day's hectic pace beginning to catch up with them. Frank Johnson was reading the front section of the paper when he suddenly looked across at Blair and grinned. "You're still getting the *Tribune,* honey? Does Cameron know you read the competition?"

"Oh, yes," Cameron replied sourly before she could say

anything. "Blair hasn't exactly made it a secret that she prefers Stan's paper to mine."

"That's not true," Blair objected indignantly. "I just haven't gotten around to subscribing to the *Gazette*."

"Frankly," her father admitted, "I'm glad to see the *Gazette* making a comeback, but I imagine the *Tribune*'s giving you quite a fight." He cast a keen eye on Cameron. "Are you going to win?"

"I'm giving it my best shot," Cameron stated firmly. "In fact, I'm starting a new advertising campaign on the first of the year to increase subscriptions. Radio, television, the whole nine yards. We've got to get some of the *Tribune*'s readership." He turned to Blair. "That's not privileged information. I want Stan to know I'm taking off the gloves in this fight."

"Then you'll have to tell him yourself," Blair retorted, irritation glittering in the emerald depths of her eyes. "I'm not running a messenger service for either one of you. I told you that, Cameron. Stan took advantage of our friendship. Why won't you believe me?" The doorbell rang and she frowned in annoyance. "I'll get that and then we can settle this once and for all."

When she returned to the living room it was with a look of embarrassed surprise on her face, and Stan at her heels.

"Speak of the Devil," Cameron said mockingly.

Blair glared at him. "Stan just dropped in to wish us all a Merry Christmas," she told her parents.

"Actually we were just discussing you," Cameron said after the Johnsons had greeted his former friend.

Stan's eyebrows shot up warily. "Oh?"

"Yeah. I don't particularly like the idea of your using a tip from my wife for a story. Especially when she asked you not to."

Blair moved closer to Cameron, not liking at all the look in his eyes. "Cameron..." she began warningly.

"I apologized for that, not that it's any of your business," Stan said coldly. "I'd say we're about even. I didn't like you handpicking some of my best employees to try to save that rag you bought, either."

Cameron's face settled into rock-hard lines. "That has nothing to do with Blair. You make sure you don't take advantage of her again."

"I already promised her I wouldn't repeat my mistake, although I wouldn't go so far as to call it 'taking advantage.' But I'm warning you, Cameron, you're the competition, and I'll use any means possible to beat you at your own game." He turned to Blair, his smile apologetic. "Sorry, Blair, I didn't mean to disrupt your holiday."

The silence after Stan's leave-taking fairly throbbed with tension. Margaret Johnson finally asked soberly, "Would either one of you like to explain what that was all about?"

"Blair will tell you," Cameron replied. "I'm taking Julie out to walk the puppies."

Blair watched them leave, her frustrations mounting with every breath she took. Unable to sit still, she paced restlessly before the fire, telling her parents the story in short, jerky sentences. When she finished she was near tears. "I've told Cameron what happened, and Stan just admitted he was in the wrong. But it doesn't seem to matter. Cameron doesn't quite believe me, even though I can tell he wants to."

"He's been hurt," her father replied quietly. "Give him some time. He'll come around."

"Everything's such a mess," she sighed, impatiently wiping at the single tear that escaped her lashes to slide down her cheek. "Stan's striking out at Cameron in every way he knows how because he's so jealous he can't see straight. But he'd die before he'd admit it."

"Jealous?" her mother exclaimed in surprise. "Why in the world would he be jealous?"

Blair sank into an armchair and leaned her head back wearily. "Because of Valerie Roland. She was with the *Tribune* for about four months and made no secret of the fact that she was attracted to Stan. But he would hardly give her the time of day. He'd been burned once by someone else pretending to be in love with him just to get a better position at the paper, and he flatly refused to let it happen again. I guess Valerie realized she wasn't getting anywhere, so she gave up. When Cameron bought the *Gazette,* she went with him."

"And Stan didn't try to stop her?" her mother asked in surprise.

"Oh, he tried to keep his star reporter, but Valerie didn't want more money. She wanted Stan." Blair sighed again. "If Valerie and Stan could come to some sort of understanding, I just know Stan and Cameron wouldn't let the competitive position of their papers come between them. They've been friends for too long. But Stan is so damn stubborn."

"So go around him," her mother suggested. "Go to Valerie. She's not a co-worker anymore. She may have no idea why Stan didn't give her any encouragement. Why don't you tell her?"

Why hadn't she thought of that? It could solve everything—or most everything. She grinned at her parents, excitement suddenly dancing in her eyes. "I think I'll do that, Mother. If anyone can possibly put an end to this bitterness between Stan and Cameron, it's Valerie Roland."

- 8 -

BLAIR HUDDLED IN her coat, cursing the icy wind that played with her gray wool suit and ran around her bare legs, her steps quickening as Quincy Market's copper dome came into view. Tilting her dove-gray hat to a cocky angle, she tried to control wisps of sandy-colored hair that kept whipping into her eyes, and finally gave up as she neared the long rectangular building where she was to méet Valerie. Faneuil Hall Marketplace. There was no better place in Boston to shop, eat or mix with people, and she loved it. The market's three five-hundred-foot buildings were packed with restaurants, specialty shops and clothing stores, and just stepping inside its gates was exhilarating. She lifted her face and sniffed the air as the varied scents of the food stands—for which Quincy Market was famous—teased her empty stomach. Pizza, chicken, seafood, cheeses—the selection was endless, and she was starved. Where was Valerie?

Wryly, Blair had to admit that the other woman hadn't

been exactly overjoyed to hear from her. In fact, she had been downright cool. Valerie had used every conceivable excuse to avoid lunching with her until Blair had made it clear that she was willing to wait as long as necessary to get an appointment. In the end Valerie had consented to meet her, although she had made no secret of her reluctance. Blair really wouldn't be surprised if Valerie was late in the hopes that Blair would get discouraged and leave.

A crowd rushed in, drawing Blair's attention from the pizza stand directly behind her, and she scanned the group anxiously. She spotted Valerie almost immediately. Tall and pencil-slim, Valerie was the type of woman that stood out in a crowd, her coal-black hair and sapphire eyes drawing all eyes to her, although Valerie never seemed aware of this fact. Her quiet confidence and cool reserve were more than a little bit intimidating. Despite the sophisticated midnight-blue wool slack suit she wore with a multicolored silk blouse, her elegance was inborn, almost casual. She'd look just as beautiful in jeans and a sweat shirt, though Blair couldn't picture her ever being quite that casual.

Lord, Blair thought as she smiled and waved, how am I going to ask her about Stan? She'll probably tell me off or freeze me with those eyes of hers. Valerie Roland had a reputation for saying what she thought.

"I'm sorry I'm late," Valerie said as soon as she reached Blair. "Have you been waiting long?"

"Not really," Blair replied. "How much time do you have? If you have to rush back to the paper, we can grab something at one of the food stands. Otherwise, why don't we try one of the restaurants?"

Valerie hesitated, her eyes cautious as they rested on Blair. "No, there's no hurry. What do you want to talk to me about?"

"Why don't we discuss it over lunch?" They moved down the central aisle of the market, wending their way through the noon crowd, and finally selected a delicatessen. Once they were seated, Blair asked lightly, "How do you like your new job?"

The older woman sipped at the coffee the waitress had brought them, her expression wary. "Is that why you called me? You want to discuss the *Gazette?*"

"Well... no." Blair stirred her coffee, searching for the best way to broach the subject of Stan. Valerie Roland wasn't the type of woman who would tolerate interference in her private life, and this conversation could well be over before it began. "I really wanted to discuss Stan." She winced as the woman seated across from her visibly stiffened, but Blair determinedly forged ahead. "I know this is none of my business, and I wouldn't be the least bit surprised if you told me to butt out. But Stan's miserable; he and Cameron are at each other's throats, and I'm caught in the middle. You could clear it all up, if you would."

"I could clear it up?" she exclaimed, startled. "How could I possibly...?"

"Are you in love with Stan?" Blair interrupted quietly.

The cool reserve that masked the other woman's emotions wavered for just an instant before she countered, "Are you?"

Blair blinked. "Am I what?"

"Are you in love with Stan?"

Blair choked, setting her coffee cup down with a clatter. "Of course not!"

"Then don't you think it's time you stopped leading him on?" Valerie demanded almost angrily. "Or are you the type of woman who goes after every man she sees? If you are, I don't know how Stan and Cameron can both be so blind."

Blair could feel her temper begin to boil. Hastily she put a lid on it. This was not the time to blow up. She studied Valerie shrewdly. "Why did you leave the *Tribune?*"

"There were several reasons," the other woman replied stiffly. "I wanted to help Cameron rebuild the *Gazette*..."

Blair shook her head, a knowing smile tugging at the corners of her mouth. "Stan and Cameron may have swallowed that, but I'm not so gullible. You were falling in love with Stan, but you thought he loved me, didn't you?"

"Yes," Valerie replied simply. "It was fairly obvious to

just about everyone. I stayed as long as I could, but Stan made it clear he wasn't interested in anyone else. So I left."

The waitress chose that moment to bring them their order, and Blair waited impatiently for the woman to leave before exclaiming, "Do you honestly think Stan would let himself fall in love with his best friend's wife? He's never, ever, shown anything for me beyond friendship."

"What was I supposed to think?" Valerie asked defensively. "I hadn't been working there a week when I realized what was going on. I heard all the stories about how he helped you start Maid-In-Heaven and gave you the emotional support you needed while your *ex*-husband was across the Atlantic. Of course I thought he was in love with you."

"I never dreamed..." Blair suddenly started to laugh, but hastily apologized when Valerie frowned. "I'm sorry. I wasn't laughing at you, just at the situation. You left the *Tribune* because you thought Stan loved me, but all the time he was crazy about you."

"Are you kidding?" Valerie scoffed, clearly disbelieving. "Stan showed me no more attention than he would a typewriter. And I did everything but jump the poor man. No, Blair, you're dead wrong. He didn't know I was alive."

"Oh, yes he did," Blair argued. "I know he puts on a great act, but he's not made of stone. He was just determined not to let you use him."

"Use him! But how—?"

"He's the owner's son," Blair reminded her softly. "You're not the first woman on the staff to show an interest in him. The last time it happened, he was hurt—badly. He swore then he'd never look at a woman on his father's payroll again."

"But that's crazy," Valerie retorted impatiently. "I couldn't care less who his father is. I don't need his help with my career. My interest in him has nothing to do with that."

"But in his eyes you were interested *because* of your career," Blair explained, sighing in relief as the wariness in Valerie's blue eyes gradually gave way to hope. "Stan has always been a little sensitive about his father. He learned the hard way not to trust everyone who approaches him in search of friendship."

"And all this time I thought he just wasn't interested. I think I could have been stark naked and he wouldn't have batted an eye."

"I doubt that," said Blair, laughing. "And he did notice your absence." When Valerie looked at her in surprise, she said, "You must have noticed the war going on between Stan and Cameron. Stan's been really hostile, striking out with every weapon he's got, and he doesn't care if he fights fair or not. He wouldn't get this upset over the loss of a city editor."

"Oh, I could strangle that man!" Valerie cried. "When I think of the times I asked him out for drinks and he put me off with one excuse after another...so all the time he thought I was trying to get in good with him because of who he is? That jerk. He let me leave without a word, and now he's taking out his frustrations on Cameron."

"Something has to be done before he destroys their friendship."

"I agree," Valerie said, "but what? I've done everything but trip the man to let him know I'm interested. And he still suspects my motives."

"Maybe he'd be more receptive now that you're not on the staff," Blair suggested gently. Thoughtfully she tapped her fingers on the tabletop. "Stan won't let down his defenses easily, that much I know. If only you could run into each other on neutral ground, you might be able to convince him that he misjudged you."

Valerie shook her head. "There's not much chance of that. We don't travel in the same circles."

"I could always invite you both to dinner," Blair suggested jokingly. Then her eyes widened and she smiled happily. "That's it! I can make myself scarce in the kitchen and leave you two alone. It'll be perfect!"

"As long as he doesn't turn around and walk out the minute he sees me."

"He won't," Blair assured her. "Are you busy Saturday night?" At the reluctant shake of Valerie's head she said,

"Then Saturday night it is. You be at my house at seven-thirty and we'll just see if Stan is made of stone. And wear something sexy."

Blair returned to her office in high spirits, a wide grin on her face, laughter spilling from her eyes for the first time since Christmas. The shadow of the hurt Cameron had been dealt over the "tip" to Stan had stood between them like a brick wall for the past two weeks. Cameron doubted her and it tore at her heart, wounding her. Come Saturday night, though, she was going to tear down that wall. Stan would rediscover Valerie, and Cameron would see he had no reason to doubt Blair. He had to!

Caroline greeted her with the mail and messages, her keen eyes immediately noting the sparkle that lunch had brought to Blair's eyes. Mischief flashed in a broad smile. "I didn't know you were meeting Cameron for lunch."

"I didn't," Blair said lightly. "I met a friend."

"Male or female?" the older woman asked just as lightly.

Blair couldn't help but laugh. "Female. You needn't worry, dearest. I haven't found a new man."

"I didn't think you had," Caroline said in an injured tone that was belied by the sparkle in her eyes. "After watching you work with some very tempting bachelors over the past two years, I know there's only one man for you. And you've already married him once. You're still in love with Cameron, Blair, and I just wanted to make sure you realized it."

Blair groaned. "I must be as transparent as glass."

"Pretty close," her friend agreed. "Do you intend to tell me what you're up to?"

"Not just yet," Blair hedged. "It's still in the planning stages." She took the mail from Caroline and flipped casually through it, then grimaced. "I didn't realize getting a group insurance plan for the company would be so complicated. Just when I think I've gone through all the company brochures, the mail brings more. I don't know if I'll be through screening it all before the next staff meeting or not. And speaking of staff, how are the two new girls working out?"

"Not bad," Caroline said. "They haven't had any problems so far, but they won't be out on their own until next week. That'll be the true test." She stopped short halfway out of the office. "Oh, Mr. Clawson also called. He said he wouldn't be needing our services for a while. I wonder why."

"I think he's had some financial setbacks," Blair said quietly. Of course, she hadn't told Caroline what she had overheard at Kenneth Clawson's house, having made one too-costly mistake in that regard already. Thankfully, neither her name nor that of Maid-In-Heaven had entered into the investigation of the bid-rigging scandal. Undoubtedly, Mr. Clawson was suspending use of her service because of the precarious state of his finances. There had been a hefty fine and the loss of several construction jobs that had been illegally obtained. All that was fine with Blair. She didn't need his type as clients.

The afternoon sped by. At last, when she was fairly sure that Stan would be in his office, she called him. Laughter bubbled up in her throat, threatening her sense of control. But she swallowed it, even though she couldn't wipe away the silly grin that had been on her face since lunch. Thank the Lord he couldn't see her! "Hi, Stan. Can I take you away from your work for a minute?"

"Anytime." He laughed pleasantly. "What's up?"

"I was hoping you could come to dinner Saturday night."

"What's the occasion?"

"Nothing special," she lied. "I just need to talk to you, so I thought we could have dinner. Can you come?"

"I don't see why not. What time?"

She sighed in relief and told him, finally hanging up with a smug smile on her face. Things were working out nicely. Stan and Valerie would soon settle things between themselves, and Cameron would see that she had never given him reason to mistrust her. Her mistake had been in forgetting that Stan was a reporter. She wouldn't do that again.

Caroline stuck her head around the door a few minutes later. "Cameron's on line one."

Blair reached for the phone eagerly, her heart jumping, even though she had just talked to him the day before. Would she always react that way? "Cameron?"

"Hi, Blair." His deep voice seemed to stroke her senses with its husky intimacy. "Are you busy?"

"Up to my ears," she chuckled, grimacing at the insurance brochures on her desk. "Why?"

He hesitated and finally said gruffly, "I need to see you. Is there any way you can get away for a while?"

The seriousness of his tone alarmed her, and she gripped the phone tighter. "What is it? What's wrong?"

"I'd rather not talk over the phone. Do you think you could come to my office?"

"I'll be right there," she assured him, fear thickening her voice. Was it Julie? Something had to be terribly wrong!

She ran from her office, slipping on her coat and searching for her keys with suddenly fumbling fingers. At Caroline's startled expression she explained, "I'm going over to the *Gazette*. I don't know when I'll be back."

"What's wrong?" Caroline cried after her retreating back.

"I don't know!" she tried not to panic, tried not to let her imagination run away with her, but she failed miserably. By the time she had reached the *Gazette*, her face was white, her stomach tied in knots. Cameron's secretary told Blair that Cameron was waiting for her.

Needing no further encouragement, she rushed into his office with little more than a perfunctory knock. She immediately spied him standing at the window and felt her heart stop at the sight of him. He looked impossibly sexy in a beige blazer and blue shirt, his oatmeal-colored slacks hugging his slim hips and flat stomach, emphasizing the long length of his legs. His eyes were dark and mysterious, flickering with fire, weakening her knees. She stepped toward him, seeking his warmth. "Cameron, what's wrong?"

A slow, languid smile spread across the chiseled planes of his face as he came slowly toward her, generating a breathlessness she had no control over. When he was just inches away, the spicy scent of his cologne calling to her senses, he lifted her chin with one hand while his other arm drew her purposefully to him. His head lowered and blocked out the world, the unexpected sweetness of his mouth feathering across hers to catch at her heart and bring tears to her eyes. Lord, how she needed this man, she thought in wonder. No one else would do for her—ever. In a hundred lifetimes she wouldn't be able to get enough of him.

She clutched at him, her arms slipping around his waist to hold him fast, her lips clinging to his. "What's wrong?" she asked against his mouth, her voice rough with love.

"Nothing, now," he growled, molding her to him, his hands treasuring the feel of her even through the thickness of her coat. His lips slid along her cheek to her ear, his teeth nibbling at her earlobe hungrily before gently teasing it with his tongue. "I couldn't wait another minute to see you." His hot breath rippled across her soft skin, causing a growing excitement.

Blair drew back to stare at him, amazement momentarily striking her speechless. Pleasure, indignation, and amusement warred with each other within her. Amusement eventually won out. "You had me run over here like some sort of idiot because you *missed* me?" she cried, her grin breaking free despite her best attempt to appear reproving. "Cameron Wakefield, you are the most—"

"Wonderful," he supplied, pressing a lingering kiss to the corner of her mouth.

She shut her eyes weakly, a smile pulling at her mouth. "Wonderful," she agreed breathlessly.

"Lovable," he coaxed, his mouth caressing her brow.

"Lovable," she said dutifully, her lips pressed lazily against his mouth.

"The most romantic man you ever had the good fortune to meet," he suggested, his voice a whisper.

"Oh, yes!" she breathed, his eyes shiny as her coat fell magically open and his hands slipped under her gray suit jacket to slide over the softness of her red silk blouse. She arched against him and laughed softly. "What am I going to do with you?"

He peered down into her eyes. "I can think of at least a dozen things. Are you open to suggestions?"

"That depends. What did you have in mind?" When he

looked pointedly toward the couch, her eyes followed his and she immediately backed out of his arms. "Oh, no!"

"I didn't think you'd go for that," he said ruefully. "It doesn't really appeal to me, either, but I'm desperate. Honey, when can we be together?"

"I thought you were going to give me some time," she reminded him.

"That was weeks ago. I thought I'd get to see more of you after Christmas, but nothing's changed. What with hiring new employees, working on the books, and looking for a hospitalization plan for the company, you're busier than ever."

"You haven't exactly been twiddling your thumbs either," she said defensively. "You've taken a personal interest in the reader poll you ran last week, you've canceled several of our evenings together because of staff meetings, and Julie hasn't seen you in over a week. And you say *I'm* busy!"

Cameron's dark brow lowered threateningly. "Don't start, Blair."

"I didn't start anything," she said tightly. "You did. I'm supposed to be at your beck and call whenever the mood strikes you, but God forbid I should expect the same of you. Is that how it works?"

"No! Dammit!" he shouted angrily, his fists clenched at his sides. "That's not how it works. Quit twisting my words!"

Blair paled, her startled eyes flying to his. She stepped back warily.

"Oh, hell!" he swore softly, the muscle in his jaw rippling as he strove for control. His fingers threaded through his hair impatiently. "I'm sorry, honey. I shouldn't have yelled at you. It's just that you've got me so tied up in knots, I can't think straight."

Blair considered him silently for a minute and then shook her head. "No, it's more than that. Are you having problems with the paper?"

"Not yet."

She frowned. "What do you mean, 'not yet'?" The paper couldn't be on the verge of failing, she thought wildly. If

Made in Heaven 145

she had a choice of the better of two evils, she'd rather have him wrapped up in his work there in Boston than in some foreign city, chasing down the news. "What haven't you been telling me? And if you dare bring up Stan's name, I swear I'll hit you!"

He ignored the jibe. "Next week we're going to print a morning and afternoon edition. Our market studies have shown that there's a need for an afternoon paper."

"Do we have a large enough populace to support three editions a day?" she asked worriedly.

"I hope so," he replied solemnly. "For the first week we'll be throwing in the afternoon edition, free, on all our paper routes."

She sank into the nearest chair, unable to believe she had heard him correctly. "You're giving it away?" she squeaked.

He nodded. "That's right."

"But that's going to cost you a fortune!"

"Not quite, but close enough," he admitted dryly. "Still, we can't sell papers if people won't read them. Giving them away is one way to make sure they're read. Hopefully it'll also increase subscriptions and advertising revenues."

"But aren't you taking an awful gamble?" Scenes of Cameron bankrupt and destitute flashed before her eyes and horrified her. She knew his family had money, but could he personally afford to throw away such large sums? "I don't want to be the one to throw a wrench in the works, but if this little experiment of yours doesn't pay off, you could lose your shirt. Can you afford it?"

His mouth lifted in a wry grin. "Would you bail me out if I couldn't?"

She wouldn't even think twice about it. "You know I would if I could. Why? Do you need money?"

He laughed, perching on the arm of her chair. "Don't worry, sweetheart, I'm not asking you to invest. My mother's already done that, though heaven help her if Dad finds out." He stroked her hair. "No, I don't need money. I need you. Would you go away with me this weekend?" he asked gruffly. "Just the two of us. I need some time to relax before the next edition hits the streets. I want to spend that time with you."

Blair's throat was suddenly desert-dry. Why this weekend? her heart cried out silently. Was Fate deliberately throwing obstacles in their way? "Cameron... I really would love to spend the weekend with you," she began hesitantly, her eyes pleading for his understanding. How could she refuse him again? she thought helplessly.

"Why do I sense a *but* here?" he growled, his eyes fierce. He got to his feet, his angry strides quickly putting distance between them. When he whirled to face her, his eyes were accusing. "You have to work this weekend, don't you?" Her guilty expression said it all, and he swore furiously. "Dammit, Blair! Why? When it comes to a choice between me and that damn company of yours, I always get the short end of the stick. I'm getting damn tired of it, too!"

"If you'd just let me explain—"

"There is no explanation," he snapped. "The bottom line is you're going to work this weekend rather than spend the time with me. You don't need to explain. I'm not dense."

"And neither am I," she cried, her own anger rising, outrage bringing her to her feet. "*I* didn't need explanations when we were married. Remember? *I* was childish when I couldn't understand why your work was more important than my birthday. *I* was supposed to understand when you weren't here to go to Lamaze classes with me and I had to go with my mother instead." The hurt she had denied for years welled up and burst free, the intensity of its escape leaving her shaking. She glared at him. "I was supposed to accept your work schedule, no questions asked. Will you tell me one thing?" she demanded. "Why the hell is it so different when we're talking about my work instead of yours?"

Her furious diatribe left him speechless. She hated herself for losing control, hated the silent tears that coursed down her cheeks. He reached for her. "Blair, honey..."

"Don't 'Blair, honey' me!" she choked out, stepping away from him to impatiently wipe the hot tears from her cheeks. "You're not going to console me with few hugs and kisses."

His hands dropped to his sides, his eyes narrowing dangerously. "Is that what you think I'm trying to do?"

"I don't know," she answered, her voice catching painfully. She buttoned her coat with trembling fingers, painfully aware of his brooding eyes on her. When she at last had her armor carefully in place, she threw her head up and met his glare defiantly. "I'm going home."

"And your answer is still no for the weekend?" he demanded.

She gripped the shoulder strap of her purse fiercely, itching to close her fingers around his throat. How could such an intelligent man be so stupid? she wondered wrathfully. Did he work at it or did she bring out the worst in him? "That's right," she agreed coldly. "And don't hold your breath waiting for an explanation. You're not going to get it."

She was almost to the door when he caught up with her. His hand closed around her arm like a steel trap and he spun her around to face him, his expression ominous. Blair shrank back in alarm, terrified that she had pushed him too far. His jaw hardened like granite and he gave her an impatient shake.

"Don't look at me like that. I'm not going to beat some sense into you, though you could certainly use it." He released her as if he couldn't stand to touch her, but his eyes still held her captive. "We're going to get a few things straight before you leave. You've used up every excuse in the book to put me off since I returned home. I'm not an unreasonable man. I knew you were still hurt and you needed time to adjust. But you're pushing me now, Blair, and I don't like it. I'm giving you fair warning: Time is running out."

She stepped back, her wide eyes searching his face. "For whom?"

He didn't even bother to answer her. "Your evasive tactics are wearing thin. I'll only accept no so many times before I take matters into my own hands."

Her eyes narrowed. "Is that a threat?"

"No, sweetheart," he said softly, a devilish glint in his eyes, "that's a promise."

Seething at his arrogance, Blair stormed out of his office. A promise, indeed! she fumed. Did he think she had no say in the matter? She wasn't a puppet he could manipulate at will!

Moments later she slammed into the office and Caroline's head jerked up in surprise. "Uh-oh. What did Cameron do this time?"

"Don't ask," Blair snapped, jerking her coat off and hanging it in the closet. "I don't want to talk about Cameron Wakefield."

"Fine," Caroline agreed, laughter dancing in her eyes. "A Mr. Simpson called..."

"I could absolutely wring his neck!"

Caroline's eyebrows shot up. "Mr. Simpson's?" she asked innocently.

"No! Cameron's."

"I thought you didn't want to talk about him."

"I don't." Angrily she flounced down in a reception-room chair and glared at Caroline when she grinned broadly. "Dammit, Caroline, this is not funny!"

"It is from where I'm sitting," her friend contradicted her. "Do you want to talk about it?"

"No. Yes! I don't know what I mean," she wailed. "I just know I'm so mad right now, I could spit nails!"

"And I thought you were just full of hot air," Caroline cracked. "Spit away if it'll make you feel better."

"That's the trouble," she said mournfully. "It won't." She sighed heavily. "He's being totally unreasonable. When he calls he expects me to drop everything and come running."

"You did a pretty fair imitation of that earlier," the older woman pointed out.

Blair groaned. "Don't remind me. I went tearing over there like an idiot, thinking he was hurt or something, and he just wanted to see me."

"What's so bad about that? The man's crazy about you."

"He's only looking after his own self-interest," Blair said flatly. "He accused me of choosing work over him, and he's not going to put up with it for much longer."

"Sounds like caveman tactics to me," Caroline laughed.

"That's what I thought."

"Enjoy it while it lasts." Blair's eyes widened and Caroline grinned. "I bet Cameron would make a great caveman. Can't you just see him in an animal skin?"

Blair laughed, her attempt to appear outraged a total failure. "Caroline, you're incorrigible."

"I know. Now that you're in a better mood, would you like to hear about Mr. Simpson?" At Blair's nod she explained, "He's a widower and he'd like us to help arrange his daughter's wedding. She's nineteen, and he needs someone to give her the advice and support a mother would. He was also hoping we could help keep a lid on expenses."

"Why doesn't he hire a bridal consultant?" Blair asked. "They're the experts at this sort of thing."

"Too expensive," Caroline explained. "And he feels a rent-a-wife would protect his interests, whereas a bridal consultant wouldn't."

Blair chewed her bottom lip thoughtfully. "Doesn't the girl have any relatives who could help her with this?" Caroline shook her head and Blair sighed. "I guess we could give it a try. But first I want to speak to Mr. Simpson to get all the details. I also want him to understand that we've never done anything like this before."

The following afternoon, after a lengthy discussion with Carl Simpson and his daughter, Brenda, Blair agreed to take care of all the details for the wedding, which would take place in April. She was in the process of going through bridal magazines when Caroline informed her she had a call from Mary Whitaker. She punched line one and lifted the receiver. "Mary, how are you?"

"That depends," Cameron's godmother replied gruffly. "I need a favor."

"Name it. You know I'll help if I can," Blair assured her.

"You may not after you hear what I want," she said in a voice as dry and rough as sandpaper. "The couple who act as caretakers for my home near Concord is leaving on a week's vacation next Monday, and I was hoping I could convince you to house-sit for me." She laughed self-deprecatingly. "You probably think I'm a foolish old woman to worry about a house so, but this was the first place Edward and I bought after we married. I've been in a tizzy over fear that something would happen to it if I left it empty a whole week. There have been several robberies in the neighborhood, and..."

"But, Mary," Blair interrupted, "couldn't one of your friends do it?"

"None would," she replied. "Not that I blame them. It's lonely out there, and they're all too old to be shoveling snow and carrying firewood. I need someone young. I thought you'd be perfect."

Blair reached for the employee work schedule and studied it quickly. "Well, I suppose Gina could do it, but I'd have to clear it with her first—"

"No! I want *you* to do it. I wouldn't trust anyone else."

"But I can't leave the office for a week," Blair exclaimed. "All my employees are trustworthy."

"I'm sure they are," Mary replied. "But I don't know them, and I'd rather not have strangers in my house."

Blair wavered. "I really would like to help you, but I just don't see how I can. Right now I have more work than I can handle..."

"Of course. I understand," the older woman replied stiffly, hurt lacing her words. "If you can't do it, there's nothing else to discuss."

"Mary, wait!" All the affection and gratitude she had had for this woman in the past came struggling to the surface, and Blair knew she couldn't turn her down. Somehow she would rearrange her schedule. "I'll do it."

"Are you sure? I don't want to push you into anything."

"I'm sure," Blair assured her, amusement suddenly dancing in her eyes. If she didn't know better, she'd swear she'd just been conned.

"I know you're busy, but his means so much to me. And I'll definitely make it worth your while." She named a sum that robbed Blair of breath and asked, "Is that enough? I want to be fair."

"That's too much," Blair choked.

"No it's not," Mary said stubbornly. "You're giving me peace of mind, and that doesn't come cheap. Now, when can you leave?"

"Monday morning, I suppose," Blair said. "I'm tied up this weekend."

"Monday will be fine. Would you like my chauffeur to drive you?"

"No, I don't think so," Blair refused. "I'd rather have my own wheels."

"Well, then, I'll send someone over with the key and directions later in the week. And, Blair, thank you. You won't regret this."

- 9 -

A MAP AND key to Mary's house was duly delivered by her chauffeur, but by late Saturday afternoon Blair had ceased to worry about the madness that had driven her to agree to the old woman's request. Instead she was overcome by an anxiety attack that showed no sign of abating as the clock drew closer to seven-thirty. Blair worked frantically to prepare for her dinner party. Dear Lord, what if she'd been wrong about Stan's feelings for Valerie? Stan hadn't mentioned the reporter in weeks. His feelings could have changed. He could have found someone else. Blair must have been crazy to think that she could pull this off!

She stepped into the living room to check the small round table she had set up by the fireplace, her nervous fingers smoothing the tablecloth, adjusting the silverware. She had to admit that she had outdone herself in making the setting romantic. The fire burning in the hearth spilled golden warmth into the room, the crackling flames providing cozy background music. The table was set with her best china and crystal, and from the center glowed a candle protected by a hurricane globe. It was beautiful, but if she had made a mistake, Stan was going to kill her.

And she'd have to think of another way to arrive at an agreement with Cameron. Time was growing short as it was. She had seen the impatience in his eyes. He was watching, waiting, playing a cat-and-mouse game that was driving her quietly out of her mind. His control had to be stretched to the limits; she knew hers was.

And yet, she wanted no shadows, no doubts between them, she thought as she went upstairs to change. Once he understood that he could trust her implicitly, once she made her position about her work—and his work—clear to him, they could settle their differences. He just had to accept the fact that she was not the dependent child he had married, willing to accept the crumbs of his time that he reserved for her. She wanted more!

The black jump suit she slipped into hugged her figure nicely, the tailored stand-up collar flattering the lines of her neck, the darkness of the material in stark contrast to the paleness of her skin and the blond highlights of her hair. She considered pulling the silky strands into a topknot, but rejected the idea with a rueful grin. Her role tonight was to promote a romance, not draw attention to herself. Once Valerie arrived, Stan probably wouldn't notice if Blair was dressed like a bag lady!

Her nerves were skittish, her movements jerky, when she returned to the living room to select the music that would make the mood perfect. When the doorbell rang she jumped and hurriedly put the records down. At the sight of Stan standing outside the door, his khaki overcoat hanging open to reveal a kelly green knit shirt and tan slacks, she flashed him a bright smile. Tall and lanky, a wide grin on his face and his red hair boyishly disarrayed, he never failed to make her laugh. She hoped the evening would put an end to the coldness between him and Cameron. "Hi! Come on in."

He whistled softly, his eyes appreciative as they swept over her. "You look great! What's the special occasion?"

Blair hung his coat in the closet and turned to grin at

Made in Heaven

him. "It's nothing special. I just wanted to wear something comfortable." She motioned him into the living room as she headed for the kitchen. "Fix yourself a drink while I check the steaks. Oh, and would you put some music on? Anything you like will be fine."

"Sure."

The strains of a romantic ballad soon floated into the kitchen, and Blair found herself humming, a smug smile playing about her mouth. Next to Cameron, Stan was the most romantic man she knew. He'd never be able to resist candlelight, music, and Valerie. The poor man didn't stand a chance.

She turned the steaks and returned to the living room to find him stoking up the fire. "I hope you're not starving to death. It'll be a while before dinner's ready."

"I can wait," he replied absently, his eyes thoughtfully studying the elegance of the table before lifting inquiringly to her face. "Why the fancy table? And the three places? Are you expecting someone else for dinner?"

The moment of truth, Blair thought. "Well, yes," she admitted reluctantly. "But please don't ask me any more questions. It's a surprise."

That, of course, was the wrong thing to tell a reporter, but she had to admit that he showed remarkable restraint. All he asked was "Where's Julie?"

His changing of the subject made her almost giddy with relief. "She and the puppies are spending the night with my parents." She chuckled. "I never thought I'd see the day my mother would let a dog sleep in her house. Julie's got her wrapped around her little finger and Mother doesn't even know it."

"Did you say *puppies?*" Stan asked, startled. "As in more than one?"

She nodded. "Cameron and I each bought her a puppy for Christmas. It really hasn't been as bad as I expected. They keep Julie entertained, and the three of them usually run out of energy at about the same time."

"Before or after they wear you out?" he teased. His eyes strayed to the table again before returning to her face. "Did you really need to talk to me or was that just an excuse to get me here? You haven't set me up with some blind date without telling me, have you? Have you, Blair?" he demanded when she flinched guiltily.

"Would I do something like that?" she asked innocently, deliberately widening her eyes.

"Yes, you would," he replied flatly. "And if you've fixed me up with a dog, I swear you'll never hear the end of this."

"I haven't. I promise." The doorbell rang, sending her to her feet nervously. Her eyes pleaded with his. "Whatever happens, don't get mad, Stan."

Leaving him in the living room, she hurried to the door, smiling brightly as she pulled it open. "You're late..." she chided reprovingly, only to have the rest of her greeting die in her throat. "Cameron!" He stood less than a foot away, ruggedly casual in faded jeans and a red plaid jacket, his dark hair sweeping his forehead, a slow smile deepening his dimples. Blair could only stare at him, suddenly breathless. What was he doing there?

"Hi," he said huskily, the warmth of his gaze moving over her in a physical caress. "Aren't you going to let me in?"

Blair could see all her carefully made plans going up in the smoke of bad timing. In desperation she blurted out, "What are you doing here? I thought you were going away for the weekend."

"Not without you," he replied stubbornly, his eyes studying her intently. He peered over her shoulder into the entrance hall, then back at her. "Is there any reason why I can't come in?"

He didn't leave her much choice in the matter. Mutely she held open the door for him, her frantic thoughts scurrying around in her head in alarm. Now what? she thought wildly. A very simple plan had just turned into a potentially explosive situation, and she couldn't do anything but stand by and wait for it to blow up in her face. She heard Stan's approaching footsteps and felt the blood drain from her face. She backed up against the door, her bulging eyes registering

Cameron's sudden stillness, his flaring nostrils and alert eyes sensing danger like those of a jungle cat.

"Well, who's the mystery guest?" Stan teased as he walked into the entrance hall. At the sight of Cameron his face fell into stiff lines and he turned to Blair, his expression frozen. "I'm not going to eat with him. I don't even want to talk to him."

"Who asked you to?" Cameron said rudely. He stepped around Stan into the doorway of the living room, his eyes quickly noting the fire and the candlelit table nearby, with its three place-settings. He turned back to glare at Blair. "Would you like to explain what's going on here?" he asked, unzipping his jacket as though he intended to stay for a while.

"Damn!" Blair cursed softly in frustration. "You're not supposed to be here."

"Obviously," he drawled. "But who's the third party? Julie?"

"Then why don't you get lost?" Stan suggested, ignoring his question. "Blair and I are having dinner, and you're not invited."

"Now I know why you refused my invitation for this weekend," Cameron snapped, ignoring Stan to impale her against the door with his furious eyes. "I actually believed you had to work, and all this time you were planning on seeing Stan."

"You're jumping to conclusions again," Blair warned him, anger sparking her eyes. "And they're not very complimentary, either. Believe it or not, you're quite wrong. Julie and I are not having dinner with Stan, in fact..."

"What the hell is going on here?" Stan demanded, thrusting himself between them.

Caught, Blair was forced to admit defeat. Her shoulders slumped, her gaze bouncing between the two men in search of an explanation that would satisfy both of them. She sighed heavily. "I guess I may as well tell you—"

The doorbell sliced through her words, and Blair's knees almost buckled in relief. Valerie! She whirled and yanked open the door, smiling at the woman standing calmly on the steps, her face serene, the slight tightness of her mouth the only sign of her inner agitation. Blair grinned and pulled her inside. "Where have you been?"

"The taxi driver got lost," she said breathlessly, slipping out of her coat and straightening the plum-colored silk tunic she wore over classic black silk pants. At the sight of Cameron and Stan staring at her in surprise, her eyes flew to Blair questioningly.

"All right, Blair, what's going on here?"

Cameron's low growl raised the hairs at the back of Blair's neck, but she only smiled encouragingly at Valerie and motioned her toward the living room. "Valerie, why don't you and Stan come in here? Stan will fix you a drink and you can explain your *problem* to him."

The other woman smiled stiffly. "All right. I could use a drink."

I could use one myself, Blair thought. She turned to Cameron. "And you can help me in the kitchen."

The door had barely swung shut behind them before Cameron grabbed her arm and whirled her around to face him. "What are you trying to do to me?" he thundered. "It's not enough that you're tearing my guts out by blowing hot and cold all the time; now you're conspiring with Stan to ruin me. What kind of woman are you?"

Blair stood unflinchingly in his grasp, blasted by his anger and hurt, but somehow she managed to remain calm. She smiled slightly. "You're getting all bent out of shape for nothing..."

"Nothing!" he exclaimed, outraged. "You call it nothing when you lie to me and sneak around behind my back? When you and Stan conspire to steal my city editor?"

She looked anxiously toward the door. "I haven't done any of those things. Will you please keep your voice down?" she hissed. "I'm sure Stan and Valerie can hear every word you're saying."

"Let them hear," he snapped. "It's the truth. I still can't believe Valerie would negotiate with Stan behind my back this way. You can't trust anybody in this business. They're all out for number one..."

Made in Heaven

A growing frustration coursed through Blair, straining against the feeling of helplessness that held her utterly still. Cameron hadn't lowered his voice one decibel. He was like a wounded bear bellowing over a hurt paw, and although she sympathized with him, she couldn't let him continue. If she didn't shut him up soon, she was terribly afraid he was going to say something unforgivable. In desperation she stood on tiptoe and cut off his flow of angry words with her mouth.

For one awful moment he stiffened, and time stood still. Her heart cried out in agony when he didn't respond. He stood stiffly, not bending but not pushing her away. But just as Blair moved to step back, he wrapped his arms around her, jerking her to him. His fingers threaded through her hair to hold her still as he crushed her mouth beneath his. All his frustration, all his pent-up anger, seemed to sweep over her. His lips were rough, bruising, his tongue arrogantly thrusting into the darkened recesses of her mouth, demanding a response she was more than willing to give.

His arms were more than a little desperate as they held her, and Blair reveled in the closeness, pressing against him, assuring him with her mouth, her hands, and her body that his fears were groundless. Gradually her silent message must have gotten through. She felt the anger give way to a fierce passion that threatened her own tenuous grip on reality. Slowly, reluctantly, she broke off the kiss, burying her lips against his neck when he groaned in protest. She gasped for breath and was finally able to murmur against his skin, "Valerie and Stan are in love."

"What?" He lifted his head from her hair to stare at her. "What did you say?"

She smiled, her eyes twinkling. "You heard me. Why else do you think Stan's been so hostile? You stole his girl."

"I didn't steal anyone," he denied. "Valerie came to me and asked for the job. I wasn't about to turn her down." He held her at arms' length, his forehead furrowed in a frown. "Why did Valerie leave the *Tribune* if she's in love with Stan? That doesn't make any sense."

"She thought Stan was in love with me," Blair admitted,

blushing. "It was really just a stupid misunderstanding. Valerie misread Stan's feelings for me and couldn't see any use in staying at the *Tribune,* crying her eyes out for a man she couldn't have. So she left."

"And Stan thought I deliberately enticed her away," Cameron guessed. "But why didn't he tell her how he felt instead of just letting her go?"

"He thought Valerie was hung up on his father's money, attracted to him because of who he is, not what he is. You know how touchy he is about that, Cameron. He was determined not to let her use him to further her career. So he let her go without a word, then realized he cared more than he wanted to admit. So he struck out at the one person he saw as the instigator of all his woes." She could see the understanding flare in his eyes. "That's right. The problem with the advertisers, the bid-rigging story, and the way he tricked me—he used every means at his disposal to strike back at you."

"Why didn't he tell me?" he demanded. "At least then I would have understood why he was so hostile. And I wouldn't have come down so hard on you when that damn story broke."

Her voice thickened in painful remembrance. "I couldn't believe you actually thought I would deliberately aid your competition, especially after the night we had just shared."

"Sweetheart, why do you think I was so upset?" His arms tightened around her. "I was on top of the world when I got up that morning. But when Stan sent those damn flowers and I read that card, I felt like I didn't know you at all." Laughter rumbled deep in his chest. "Damn Stan anyway! All this time I was worried he was after my woman, he was worried I was after his. It serves us right for not leveling with each other from the beginning."

"Speaking of Stan, don't you think it's time we put in an appearance? They're probably wondering what happened to us." She looked at him reflectively. "I'll have to set another place at the table. Fortunately there's plenty of steak..."

"I doubt that they've given us a thought," Cameron said

as he watched her gather an extra place setting. He held the door open for Blair to precede him.

Valerie and Stan were deep in conversation when Cameron followed Blair into the living room. At Cameron's I-told-you-so look, Blair smiled and said in a voice laced with humor, "Are you two ready to eat? The steaks are done. In fact, they're going to be tough if we don't eat soon."

The other couple exchanged a telling glance, and Stan finally said, "Would you mind if we take a rain check, Blair? We're probably being unforgivably rude, but we've got a lot of catching up to do and..."

"And you'd rather be alone," Blair supplied when he hesitated. "I don't understand it," she said, her frown belied by the twinkle in her eyes. "Every time I arrange one of these romantic dinners, nobody eats!"

"I will," Cameron exclaimed. "I'm not giving up steak for a walk in the moonlight."

Blair's eyebrows shot up. "Oh, really?"

A boyish grin flashed across his face. "Maybe I'd better rephrase that."

"That would be advisable," she agreed, "if you expect to get steak tonight. Otherwise you'll get cold turkey."

"Meaning birds of a feather," began Stan, his laughing eyes on his friend. "You know the rest, don't you, Cameron?"

"Yeah, I guess I do." He measured Stan silently for a moment. "Are you going to be on the panel at Boston College next week? The one for the journalism students?" At Stan's affirmative nod he said, "I'll see you there, then."

Blair heaved a sigh of relief. The ice was broken. They were still circling one another warily, but the element of hostility that had darkened their friendship was gone. Now, if only she and Cameron could come to terms, the evening would be perfect.

The house was unexpectedly quiet after Stan and Valerie left. Cameron followed her into the living room, his eyes twinkling as they swept around the room. "Don't you think you got a little heavy-handed with the candles and romance?" he teased. "Stan must have realized this was a setup the minute he walked in the door."

"He was sure I'd set him up with a blind date." Blair chuckled. "He wasn't happy about it at all, but Valerie changed his mind very quickly."

"Talk about taking unfair advantage! When did you get into the matchmaking business?"

"The day you came back to Boston," she retorted flippantly. "If you want your steak while you can still cut it with a knife, we'd better eat now."

He caught up with her in the kitchen. "I thought you wanted to go for a walk in the moonlight. In fact, I was sort of looking forward to it."

"That's not what you said earlier," she reminded him, smiling. "Besides, it's too cold."

"I could warm you up," he suggested lightly. "I've been told I'm very good at that."

Blair turned her back with the excuse of removing the baked potatoes from the oven and steak from the broiler, laughter sparkling in her eyes like stars. "Frankly, I'd rather eat."

"It's a sad state of affairs when you'd rather eat than take a walk in the moonlight. I must be slipping." He watched her set two plates on the kitchen table and frowned reprovingly. "You want to eat in the *kitchen?* Sweetheart, that's hardly romantic."

"Who said it was supposed to be romantic?"

"You did. Remember, you're the one who said no one ever eats your romantic dinners. And since I'm taking Stan's place . . ."

"That's why we'll eat in here. I want to make sure your mind stays on the food. Besides," she reasoned, "it's not *where* you are that's romantic but who you're with."

"Good point," he nodded, pulling out a chair from the table and motioning her into it. Once she was seated, he leaned down and kissed her shoulder. "Let's forget about Valerie and Stan and make our own romance."

And they did. With the gas burners lit on the stove and a candle stuck in the top of an empty wine bottle, they gazed into one another's eyes, laughed softly, and couldn't have

Made in Heaven

cared less that the steak was tough and dry and the potatoes baked hard. The candle flame danced in the darkness of Cameron's eyes, lighting the tenderness there, the laughter. The music was the beating of their own hearts, the words those their eyes communicated. It was a meal Blair would remember for the rest of her life and would always treasure. She hated to see it end.

They did the dishes together, arguing over who would wash and dry, and Blair had never enjoyed that hated chore more. As they stood close together at the sink, with hips and elbows occasionally meeting, Blair closed her eyes for a moment and luxuriated in the feeling of closeness. Why did everything seem so easy right now?

When the last plate was dried and put away, she turned off the stove burners while Cameron blew out the candle, and they made their way into the living room.

Cameron pulled her down next to him on the rug, their backs against the couch and legs stretched out in front of them toward the glowing embers of the dying fire. He didn't touch her except to hold her hand. For long moments the only sound was that of an occasional spark in the fireplace. Blair dragged her gaze from the hypnotic sight of the fire to find Cameron's eyes on her. A deep frown furrowed his brow, and automatically she reached up to smooth it away, her own eyes puzzled as they met his. "What's wrong?"

He leaned his head back and closed his eyes. "Nothing," he sighed. "I was just thinking." His fingers tightened around hers. "What are your plans for Maid-In-Heaven?"

"My plans?" she echoed, surprised. "I don't know. Why?"

"You must have had some long-range goals when you started the business," he persisted. "I just wondered what they were."

"Originally," she admitted candidly, "I started it because I wanted to forget you. And I wanted to work out of my home and be in business for myself, so as to spend as much time as possible with Julie."

"And did it work?"

"Did what work?" she asked, confused.

"Did it make you forget me?"

"No." If anything, it had brought him closer. When she was buying clothes for other men, when she was cooking dinner for someone else, it had been all too easy to remember doing those things for Cameron. She frowned at him. "Why the sudden interest?"

"Since your future is directly related to mine, I think it's time we decided where we're going." His eyes met hers. "Don't you agree?"

"Yes, of course," she said, her eyes searching his face. "Since you've asked about my business, you should be willing to tell me about the *Gazette*, especially since you know now that I won't be reporting back to Stan. What are your plans?"

He studied the fire broodingly, almost as if he could see into the future. "Once the *Gazette* makes it, I'm going to buy another paper on the verge of collapse. After I've put that one back on the road to success, I'll buy another and another until my company's as big as Harper Publications."

"Are you going to be another William Randolph Hearst?" she teased, hiding her uneasiness behind a quick smile. How had she ever thought he had changed? she wondered wildly. He was more ambitious than ever. He would never make those dreams a reality by staying home nights with his wife and child. No, to achieve that kind of success, he would have to court it actively.

Pain shafted through her, spurred on by the reality she had heretofore refused to acknowledge. Over the past few weeks she had deliberately chosen to ignore that fact, basking in the good times and forgetting that her relationship with Cameron was built on crumbling ground. The foundation was already beginning to crack. Was there any way to patch it?

"I can practically see the wheels turning in your head, Blair. What are you thinking?"

"What am I thinking?" She laughed, but there was no humor in the sound. "I was wondering how long it will be before you'll run off looking for another paper, and I'll have to tell you good-bye."

"That's in the distant future, and who said anything about

saying good-bye?" He got up to put a log on the dying fire and swung back to face her, taking advantage of his superior height to pin her to the floor with his eyes. "Don't you think it's time you stopped blaming me for everything and took a good hard look at yourself?"

"What do you mean?" she demanded, scrambling to her feet. "I haven't blamed you for everything..."

"Oh, come off it, Blair. My job—or rather my ambition—has always been a sore spot with you. You've continually thrown it in my face since I returned to Boston."

"And haven't I had good reason?" she cried. "I've listened to all your plans for the *Gazette* and this empire you plan to build, watched you dedicate hours to making that dream come true. Can you blame me for wondering where Julie and I will be while you're off chasing success?"

"Yes, I can," he replied stiffly. His gaze trapped hers, refusing her release. "I could be right by your side if you'd let me. But you won't. It's not my career that's keeping us apart, but yours."

Indignation flared in her eyes. "Name one time my career has kept us apart!" she challenged him.

"One? I can name at least half a dozen," he retorted. "What about Christmas Eve? What about the evening you went shopping for your client after we took Julie to see Santa Claus? I see you three nights a week, but you're always rushing off with one excuse or another as soon as we're finished eating. Whether or not you realize it, you've jumped at every possible chance to use Maid-In-Heaven as a shield against me." He eliminated the space between them with one long stride, his fingers biting into her shoulders as he held her in front of him. "You heard me and Stan talking about the panel discussion at Boston College. It's Wednesday night at eight, and I'd love to have a friendly face in the crowd. Will you come?"

"Wednesday night? Of course—" She stopped and lifted wide eyes, suddenly remembering the house-sitting job for his godmother. "I can't."

"You see," he said, his face settling into grim lines. "I could have been by your side every day, in your bed every night, but you won't let me. It's almost as if you don't want to believe that I've changed, so you go around throwing up roadblocks."

"That's not true," she whispered through suddenly dry lips. "I've made a commitment for this week. For your godmother, I might add. She wants me to house-sit for her, and I agreed. Maybe I could drive in from Concord for Wednesday night, but I'll have Julie with me. It'll be too late for her, and I'm afraid it's just too complicated. I accepted the job and I can't back out now."

"You're house-sitting for Mary?" he exclaimed, tension easing out of his face. "Then there's no problem. I'll just call her...."

"No you won't," she said flatly. "I gave my word, Cameron. I'm going."

"Come hell or high water?" he demanded coolly, his thick brows fierce. "Just listen to yourself, sweetheart. You're the one who's always saying good-bye. I've been here all along, but you refuse to accept that."

"What I refuse to accept is that a leopard can change his spots," she corrected him defensively. "You've just said yourself that you want to build a newspaper empire. That type of ambition doesn't fit in with the lifestyle I want."

"Do you think I'd be here now if I didn't want a life with you?" he demanded. "I know what *I* want, Blair. Why else do you think I accepted your constant refusals of my invitations without getting discouraged and giving up? I want you! More than a career, more than anything. And I'm not going anywhere. If I can't build the *Gazette* into a string of newspapers without leaving you, then I'll be happy with the *Gazette* alone. *As long as you're by my side.*"

She lifted swimming eyes to his. "Cameron..."

"No, let me finish," he said sternly. "*You* are the one who has to decide what you want. This blowing hot and cold all the time is driving me crazy. I can't take any more, so I'm calling a halt here and now. You've got all the time you need to decide if you want a life with me. I'm not going to torture myself anymore by trying to pressure you into my bed. When you know what you want, let me know. You know where I live."

She watched him leave, too stunned to do anything but follow him to the door. Just before he closed it behind him, his eyes met hers. "Don't make me wait too long, sweetheart. I won't wait forever."

- 10 -

"JULIE'S STAYING WITH your father and me," Margaret Johnson insisted stubbornly, her jaw set in an uncompromising line. "This isn't a vacation. You're taking a briefcase full of work, and there's no way you're going to get any of it done if you're cooped up with a four-year-old for a whole week. Why don't you leave her here, honey? We'll look after her properly."

"Mother, you know it's not that," Blair said, leaning back in her chair with a sigh. "I know you and Dad will take good care of her, but she's not your responsibility." They had been arguing for the better part of an hour without getting anywhere. Blair looked pointedly at her watch and then back at the two women camped in front of her desk. "I should have left an hour ago. What does it take to convince you two that Julie isn't any trouble? She is my daughter, you know. I'm used to looking after her."

"We're not arguing with that," Caroline replied. "But

you yourself said this house-sitting job would give you a chance to get a lot of work done. Julie is very active. Will she understand that you won't have time to entertain her?"

"Probably not," Blair admitted reluctantly. "And I do need to get some work done. Lately I just haven't been able to concentrate. I guess I've had a lot on my mind."

"I think six foot two qualifies as a lot," Caroline remarked. "You need some time alone, Blair."

Margaret Johnson rose to her feet and pulled on her coat and gloves. "Then it's settled?" At Blair's reluctant nod, she sighed. "Good. I'll pick up Julie at nursery school and come back here for the puppies. Give me a call when you get back, and I'll bring them all home." She came around the desk to kiss her daughter on the cheek. "Don't work the whole time you're gone, honey. Get some rest. You look tired."

Tired wasn't the word for it. She hadn't gotten more than two consecutive hours of sleep since Saturday night. Cameron plagued her dreams at night and distracted her during the day. Juggling her schedule to fit in the house-sitting job was a nightmare, and although she longed to call Mary and back out of their agreement, she couldn't. Mary was counting on her. She had promised, and she couldn't renege on that for Cameron or anyone else.

Caroline waited until the door shut behind the older woman before turning back to her friend. "Don't worry about the business while you're gone. The girls and I will have everything well in hand. You don't have to give us another thought."

"Caroline, this is hardly fair, you know," Blair protested halfheartedly. "Mike won't like you putting in all this time, and I don't feel right about dumping everything in your lap. I should stay here and let one of the girls go."

"You've built this company on the premise that the needs of the customer come first. Cameron's godmother wants you to do it. Anyway," she argued, "what can happen in a week? The office will run just as smoothly as it always does because you've made sure of that before you left. And you're taking so much work with you, you won't have time to give us a second thought."

"I hope so." Lord, she didn't want to think about *anything*.

"You and Cameron had a fight, didn't you?" Caroline asked quietly.

"Not exactly," Blair hedged. She got to her feet and paced restlessly about the room. "He's backing off until I decide what I want."

"And have you decided?"

"It's not that simple. There's a lot to consider."

"Not really," Caroline contradicted her with a smile. "If you love him and he loves you, that's all that really matters. The rest will work itself out."

Could things really be that simple? Blair wondered as she left Boston a short while later. There was no question in her heart or mind that she loved Cameron, and after his declaration Saturday night, she knew his feelings for her ran just as deep. So what was keeping them apart? His work? She winced. He was right. When she had allowed it, he'd been by her side as often as possible.

How his accusations haunted her! She had only been doing her job, carrying out the responsibilities she had set for herself. How could he accuse her of using Maid-In-Heaven as a shield? If she was guilty of hiding behind her work, then surely he had been guilty of the same thing during their marriage. He had no right to criticize her for something he himself had done. Had he?

Her spirits sank, her musings offering her no satisfactory answer to her problem. When she finally located Mary's house, she could only sit in her car and stare at the enormous structure. Gray siding, gray shutters, gray sky. It matched her mood exactly. The three-story edifice was a hodgepodge of additions that didn't quite match, complete with bay windows, gables, and two chimneys, and looked as if it had been around since the days of the American Revolution.

Blair got out of the car reluctantly. Rambling around in

the old house for a week would probably drive her batty, but she might as well go in and make herself comfortable. She grabbed her suitcase and stepped determinedly onto the wooden porch.

Surprisingly, though, the inside of the house was quite charming. Blair found herself wandering from room to room, inspecting a myriad intriguing nooks and crannies. Much of the furniture was antique, dark, and heavy, but in excellent condition. Although the beds were sturdy and old, she was relieved to see that the mattresses were modern. Upstairs she found a small bedroom at the back of the house that offered a breathtaking view of the Concord River. Even now, when the countryside was shrouded in snow and the naked trees pointed stark fingers into the grim sky, it was a sight she could not get enough of. She immediately chose the room for her own use for the duration of her stay.

After unpacking, she went back downstairs and found the kitchen. The departing caretakers of the estate, the Thompsons, had left the refrigerator well stocked, and there was plenty of canned goods in the pantry. But it was the fireplace in the corner, its hearth blackened with the soot of ages, that drew her attention. A fireplace in the kitchen. She could easily come to love this house.

Time passed slowly, despite the work to which she diligently applied herself. One insurance brochure soon began to look like another, the words running together to distract her. She forced herself to continue, ignoring the wind whistling around the corners of the house, closing her ears to the strange creaks and groans of her unfamiliar surroundings. By the time darkness fell, she was totally exhausted.

The following day, however, she found it impossible to avoid the thoughts that picked at her concentration. Unable to sit still, she put down the scheduling she was working on and roamed restlessly about the old house, her own footsteps mocking her. Were Caroline and Cameron right? Had she unconsciously been the one standing in the way of her own happiness?

Depression closed in on her, threatening to suffocate her.

Made in Heaven

In desperation she pulled on boots and a down-filled jacket and stepped outside. It was bitterly cold, but almost immediately the solitude of the countryside caught at her low spirits and warmed her. It was so quiet! The house was very secluded; there were no close neighbors to disturb the silence. The trees creaked in the wind, sending shivers down her spine, and she swore she could hear the ice freezing in the river. With every step she took, the snow crunched under foot. The icy wind brought tears to her eyes and burned her throat, but she only shoved her mittened hands deeper into her pockets and headed for the copse of trees along the river.

Self-analysis was the pits, she thought wryly, kicking at a clump of snow. She had been terrified of getting hurt again, of having her heart torn out by the roots when the man she loved walked away. Out of self-preservation, had she used work to protect her too vulnerable heart? God, she hadn't meant to! It hadn't even been a conscious decision. It had just happened.

And she had hated every minute that her work had come between them. Surely Cameron would believe that. Christmas Eve had been meaningless for her. Her heart had been with him the entire time, leaving an empty shell at her own party. This past weekend she had seen the disappointment in his eyes when once again she had to turn down one of his invitations, and she couldn't really blame him for thinking her work was more important to her than he was. Somehow she had to make him understand that her feelings for him and the decisions she was forced to make in her work were not even remotely related.

She stiffened, her face suddenly as white as the snow. Cameron must have often experienced the same frustration when they were married. He must have been torn by his longing to be with her and the need to make a name for himself as a reporter. In her insecurity she hadn't realized that the choices he sometimes had to make had nothing to do with his love for her, just as the choices she had made had nothing to do with her feelings for him. And all this time she had thought he loved his work more than her. Did he feel that way about Maid-In-Heaven? Dear Lord, she had to set him straight.

She practically ran back to the house, more alive than she had felt in days. She could accept his work now that she knew where she stood with him. He loved her! He really loved her, and she had almost destroyed that by her unthinking actions. She reached for the phone and stopped. No. This was not something they could discuss over the phone. Tomorrow night he would be at Boston College. He had wanted a friendly face in the crowd. It was a long drive on bad roads, but it would be worth it if she could surprise him. Surely, when he saw her there, he would know that she loved him, that he was more important than any job.

Once her decision was made, however, time dragged twice as slowly. She was gnashing her teeth in impatience when darkness finally fell and she could go to bed. But the next day she had a new worry. The National Weather Service issued a winter storm warning, and she spent the day watching the skies, too anxious about her evening plans to do anything but keep an alert eye out for the first snowflake.

The sky grew blacker, slipping into night, and when she looked out the window one final time before leaving, all she saw was her reflected image, the emerald silk blouse ruffled about her neck, the whiteness of her wool suit that made her figure so trim and petite, the wispy strands of blond hair that had escaped her sophisticated chignon. Anxiety darkened her eyes. Should she wear something less businesslike? Would Cameron spot her in the audience? Maybe she should wear her hair down. . . .

But a glance at the slim gold watch strapped to her wrist made her grab her coat and fly out the door. She hardly noticed the light snow that began to fall as she started the car. Traveling the winding roads in the dark was quite different from doing so in daylight, but eventually she made it to the main road. From there it was a straight course to Boston. Finding her way about the college campus, however, was something else entirely. She had to ask directions several times before she was able to locate the lecture hall,

Made in Heaven

and even then she wasn't sure she was in the right place until she saw Stan. She scanned the audience and grinned when she spotted Valerie seated near the back of the room. She hurried over to slip into the empty seat beside her. "Somehow I knew you'd be here," Blair said.

Valerie's blue eyes widened. "Blair! What are you doing here?"

"What do you think I'm doing here?" She laughed. "I wanted to hear Cameron's speech." The lights dimmed warningly and she asked hurriedly, "Didn't he tell you he invited me?" At the other woman's shake of her head, she shrugged. "He probably didn't mention it because I didn't think I'd be able to come. Where is he?"

"He couldn't make it."

"What!" Blair exclaimed, startled. "Why not?"

Valerie shook her head. "All he said was that he was going out of town. He won't be back at work until next week."

Blair sat stunned, her eyes hardly registering the fact that the lights had lowered and the lecture had begun. Cameron had left town without even bothering to tell her. Had he grown tired of waiting for her to come to him? She shouldn't have postponed as she did. She should have called him yesterday and explained how she felt. Now it might be too late.

She waited impatiently for the guest panelists to finish giving their speeches, tapped her foot in growing irritation during the question-and-answer period, and was a nervous wreck by the time the applause died down and Stan had come to join them. She grabbed his arm. "Stan, do you know where Cameron is? Valerie told me he's gone out of town."

He frowned and ushered them outside. "No, I don't know where he's gone. All I know is he had to cancel tonight because something important came up. He had to leave the city and he didn't know when he'd be back."

"And he didn't say where he was going?" When Stan said no, her spirits sank. "I've got to find him."

"Not tonight you won't," Stan contradicted her, glaring

at the snow swirlling around their heads. "You might as well go home, Blair. This snow's not going to let up tonight, and you can't do anything till morning anyway."

"I can't go home. I'm house-sitting in Concord." The coldness of the winter night would chill her soul, and she could only summon a weak smile "You're right. I'd better get going before the roads get any worse."

"Why don't you stay in town tonight?" Valerie suggested suddenly. "You shouldn't be driving in weather like this."

But Blair insisted, and a short while later she was back on the road to Concord. The snow already covered the highway and was piling up in drifts along the roadside. She strained to see in the darkness, turning the windshield wipers to high and praying that they wouldn't ice up on her. Her nerves were stretched as taut as a piano wire when she finally turned onto the winding road that led to Mary's house and realized just how deep the snow was on the winding little-traveled road. She slowed to a crawl, inching around the curves and holding her breath every time the rear wheel slipped. When the dark gables of the house suddenly appeared in front of her, she brought the car to a sliding halt and leaned her head weakly against the steering wheel, practically shaking in relief.

The door was jerked open, and Blair's head snapped up in surprise, her breath leaving her body in a rush at the sight of the dark giant standing before her, covered in snow. "Where the hell have you been?" he growled.

The scream rising in her throat suddenly died. Snow blew around him like a shrouding mist, clinging to his lowered brows and teak-colored hair, brushing the shoulders of his suit. His eyes were black as the night: angry, fierce. Blair swallowed weakly, her heartbeat thundering in her ears, her throat dry. Her widened eyes flew to his. "Cameron! What are you doing here?"

He ignored her question and bellowed, "Haven't you got any better sense then to drive in this kind of weather? What was so all-fired important that you had to risk your life for it on these roads?"

"You," she answered simply, her eyes glowing in the

darkness. "I went to your lecture."

"Where's Julie?"

"With my mother."

His eyes were unreadable. Reaching across her, he switched off the motor. "Come on, let's go in the house. It's freezing out here."

He ushered her inside, helping her with her coat and the jacket to her suit, running his hands over her shoulders and arms, brushing the snow from her hair. "Are you all right?" he asked gruffly, a flame of desire sparking in his eyes as they swept over her in an almost physical caress.

"I'm fine," she whispered, unable to tear her gaze away from the beloved lines of his face. Her fingers trembled with the need to soothe the frown from his brow, to slip his gray suit coat from his broad shoulders, to slyly, teasingly, unbutton each button of his gray vest and steel blue shirt. She longed to drive him crazy with desire, to set him afire, but she couldn't seem to move. She stared at him helplessly and wished he'd take her in his arms. "What were you doing outside without a coat? Trying to catch pneumonia?"

"I was mad as hell when you drove up," he said, his black eyes inspecting every inch of her with a thoroughness that left her breathless. "I didn't need a coat to keep me warm. Do you have any idea how dangerous the roads are tonight?"

"I could ask you the same thing," she countered. "What are you doing here?"

"I told you I wasn't a patient man." His husky words brushed over her with rough tenderness and wrapped around her heart. He took a step toward her. "Don't get mad, sweetheart, but you're the victim of a setup."

She frowned. "A setup? What are you talking about?"

"Mary," he answered simply. "She's been playing matchmaker again. I just found out about it this morning when she called me to tell me what she had arranged."

Blair's eyes narrowed. "What," she asked ominously, "do you mean by that?"

"Mary thought we needed some time to ourselves to work out our differences. So she arranged for the caretakers to take the week off and then pressured you to house-sit."

"I rearranged my schedule for nothing?" she demanded, her eyes glittering with golden sparks of outrage. "How could she do that to me? I don't have time for such games..."

"Her intentions were good," Cameron said defensively. "It's not her fault that they backfired."

A sudden fear grabbed Blair's heart. "Backfired?"

"She forced you to choose between me and Maid-In-Heaven," he explained. "And your choice was obvious."

"Don't be ridiculous!" The hurt that laced his voice stabbed her heart, and she knew if she didn't talk fast, she'd lose him forever. "Cameron, can't you see that my love for you goes far beyond my dedication to Maid-In-Heaven? I love *you*. Why do you think I went into town tonight? During the last few days I've realized that nothing is as important as our being together."

"Does that mean you're prepared to give up Maid-In-Heaven and have only one husband?" he demanded.

"I've always had just one husband. You."

"You're not answering my question," he retorted, frowning.

Lord, how was she going to get through to him? she wondered in growing panic. She stepped toward him until they were less than a foot apart. "When you went off to that banana republic after I got pregnant, I had to tell you about my pregnancy over the phone. Did you love me then?"

"Of course I loved you!" he snapped. "How can you ask such a stupid question?"

A soft smile played on her mouth. "And did you want to come home to be with me?"

"Of course. But you know I couldn't. I know you were hurt by it, but I was work—" The words died on his lips, understanding flaring in his eyes as they snared hers. "Did you want to be with me and Julie on Christmas Eve?" he asked.

"How can you ask such a stupid question?" she mimicked him in a voice laden with love and laughter. "It was the worst evening of my life, but I couldn't abandon my guests."

He reached for her, pulling her toward him until they

were almost but not quite touching. "Do you realize how much time we've wasted?"

She traced the curve of his brow with her finger. "It hasn't been completely wasted. We're here together now, and that's what counts." She touched the corner of his mouth, her eyes revealing all the pain of the past as they met his. "Don't ever leave me again," she whispered. "I couldn't stand it."

"Never," he breathed huskily, closing each eye with a kiss before rediscovering with delicious slowness all the delicate lines of her face. His mouth moved to her ear to bite tenderly at the sensitive lobe.

She moved against him, her hands moving over his back, luxuriating in the feel of him. His masculine scent called to her, and her body responded with a slow-burning fire that grew hotter with each touch, each kiss. Her overwhelming need for him thrived on his closeness, but before she was completely lost to reason, she drew back. "Why did you wait so long to come home?" she asked, voicing the question that had been nagging at her for a long time. "You said you realized almost immediately you'd made a mistake when you left for London without me. Why didn't you come home then?"

"It wouldn't have worked," he admitted solemnly. "We both needed time to grow up before we destroyed our love. It had gotten to the point where neither one of us could see any viewpoint other than our own. You felt threatened by my career and I couldn't understand why." He laughed softly. "Believe me, I do now!"

"But two years, Cameron! Anything could have happened. What would you have done if I'd have met and married someone else?"

He grinned, devilment dancing in his eyes. "There was no chance of that happening. Your mother was keeping me posted."

Blair digested that piece of information and laughed ruefully. "I should have known. So why did you decide this was the time for you to come back? I haven't been seeing anyone special."

"I couldn't wait any longer."

His gruff admission caught at her heart. "I'm glad. I was tired of waiting, too. Does this mean you don't doubt me anymore?"

"How can I doubt you when you went out in this storm to find me? Don't you ever do anything like that again!"

"No, sir!" She saluted him impertinently. "But it really wasn't that bad when I started out. Anyway, you're a fine one to talk. You went out in it, too."

"I wasn't going to let you get snowed in out here by yourself."

She pulled him over to the window to gaze into the snowy darkness. "Are we really going to be snowed in?"

"That depends on how long it takes the snowplows to get to these back roads. We could be stranded here for the rest of the week."

"And what about the paper? Can your employees get by that long without you?"

"They're going to have to. I took the rest of the week off." He grinned wickedly. "Anyway, I left word that I had a tawny-haired lioness to tame and not to expect me until they saw me."

"Cameron, you didn't!"

"Oh, yes I did," he laughed. "Come here, darling, and let's see how well I've tamed you."

She fell willingly into his arms, playfully sinking her nails into his back. When he winced, she growled, "Don't forget—this cat has claws."

"I wonder what it takes to make you purr, my little lioness," he said thoughtfully, sweeping her up in his arms and starting toward the stairs. "I can't wait to find out."

"That's easy," she murmured against his neck, licking him lightly and then laughing when he stiffened. "A lot of love. Think you can handle it?"

"Oh, I'm sure of it."

He carried her upstairs, into the bedroom she had been using since her arrival, and straight through to the bathroom. When he stepped into the old-fashioned clawfoot tub and pulled the shower curtain closed behind them, she lifted a

Made in Heaven 181

brow inquiringly. "What do you think you're doing?" she demanded with a hauteur that was hard to maintain above the insistent smile that was creeping across her face.

"What does it look like I'm doing? You wanted love and you're going to get it. After a shower to relax you, I'm going to put you to bed and love you till you beg me to stop."

"I'll never beg you to stop."

"We'll see."

He reached for the faucet handle and she couldn't seem to draw her eyes away. "Cameron Wakefield, don't you dare! This is—" Warm water shot over them, drowning out her words, and she screeched in protest. "This is my favorite blouse! You've ruined it!"

"Don't worry, sweetheart." He blinked the water out of his eyes. "I'll buy you another." Her released her legs and stepped back to admire her, his gaze roaming hotly over her, lingering on the way the emerald silk clung to her wet breasts. His eyes devoured her. "Maybe I won't buy you another one after all. This one looks pretty good to me."

Blair felt herself drowning in the warmth of his gaze. She brought his hand to her breast, a shuddering sigh ripping through her as his fingers sparked lightning deep inside her and desire ran through her like wildfire. Her hands went to the buttons of his vest and shirt, moving down his chest with teasing slowness. Through spiky lashes, her eyes flirted with his. "Didn't anyone ever tell you you're not supposed to shower with your clothes on?"

She pulled the clinging material from his wet back to drop it at their feet, her hands straying back to his waist to glide up his firm chest, her fingers playfully pulling at the furry mat of hair that narrowed and disappeared beneath his belt. "You feel good," she groaned, arching into him. "We should always take showers together."

"That can be arranged," he said roughly, his eyes burning black with growing passion as he stripped her wet shirt and bra from her to give his eyes free reign. "God, you're beautiful!" He leaned down to press a kiss to the throbbing pulse in her throat before letting his open mouth slip down the rounded swell of her breast to latch on to her nipple, his teeth and tongue teasing and torturing her until she was writhing in his arms.

Blair clung to him, her hands pulling at his gray slacks before sliding around to his back; then she raked her nails down his spine in a feline caress that made him groan in response. She wanted to feel him, taste him, with no barriers between them. His eyes encouraged her to strip them both of their sodden clothes. She didn't hesitate.

When she reached for the soap, he grinned. "I'm all yours, sweetheart."

She started to soap his hard body with long, sweeping strokes that lingered and worshiped, but when Cameron leaned down and covered her mouth with his in a drugging kiss that seemed to go on without end, she dropped the soap and reached for him. She was past thought, past caring about anything but him, when he released her mouth and picked up the soap. He lathered every inch of her body with infinite care, their whispered sighs mingling with the mist above their heads until they were both nearly out of their minds with desire. Just when Blair thought she couldn't stand another minute of the exquisite torture, he pulled her under the spray of water, chased the soap away with the palms of his hands, and turned off the water. He grabbed a towel, his hands brusquely rubbing her dry until she was rosy and warm, aching for a fulfillment only he could give. Her own hands lingered on his body until he impatiently tore the towel from her hands and carried her into the bedroom.

The blizzard raged outside, but no ice touched their bed; no cold could survive the blistering heat they built between them. They reveled in each other, smiling at each other's moans of pleasure, driving themselves ever closer to the edge until they fell into the flames with a muffled cry, each entwined lovingly in the other's arms.

Blair woke much later, swimming up from the depths of slumber to stretch languidly under Cameron's stroking hands. She smiled sleepily against his chest. "Don't stop."

"I don't plan to," he replied huskily. "Not in this lifetime or the next." He buried his face in her hair, inhaling the sweetness of it. "This is where you belong, sweetheart, where you've always belonged. I'll never let you go again."

"Isn't that going to be a little difficult?" she teased. "You do have a paper to run."

His arms tightened around her. "You are my life; the paper isn't. Don't ever forget that."

"And what about this empire you're going to build?" she asked softly.

"Haven't you ever heard of delegating authority?" He lifted her chin and met her eyes in the darkness. "I meant what I said about not wanting any of it if that means giving you up. Now that I've got my priorities straight, there'll be no more separations. I'm not saying there won't be late nights," he warned, "but I never again intend to spend a night without you by my side."

Blair kissed him tenderly, the love she had for him ten times stronger than the day she married him. Her eyes were dusted with starlight when they met his. "I've been thinking of making some changes in Maid-In-Heaven, too."

He stopped her with a finger across her lips. "Don't do it unless you really want to."

She grinned and kissed his finger. "You know me better than that. Actually, I was thinking of offering Caroline a partnership. Now that I'm getting my husband back, I want to spend as much time as possible with him. No more working late nights or weekends. From now on I have only one special client."

"And what about company policy?" he reminded her, a wicked glint in his eyes as his hand swept up her bare hip to capture a round breast. "It was once pointed out to me that touching and kissing clients is strictly against the rules."

"And I thought you were so smart," she murmured against his mouth. "Hasn't anyone ever told you that rules were made to be broken?"

WONDERFUL ROMANCE NEWS!

Do you know about the exciting SECOND CHANCE AT LOVE/TO HAVE AND TO HOLD newsletter? Are you on our *free* mailing list? If reading all about your favorite authors, getting sneak previews of their latest releases, and being filled in on all the latest happenings and events in the romance world sound good to you, then you'll love our SECOND CHANCE AT LOVE and TO HAVE AND TO HOLD Romance News.

If you'd like to be added to our mailing list, just fill out the coupon below and send it in...and we'll send you your *free* newsletter every three months—hot off the press.

☐ *Yes, I would like to receive your free SECOND CHANCE AT LOVE/TO HAVE AND TO HOLD newsletter.*

Name _____
Address _____
City _____ State/Zip _____

Please return this coupon to:

Berkley Publishing
200 Madison Avenue, New York, New York 10016
Att: Rebecca Kaufman

HERE'S WHAT READERS ARE SAYING ABOUT

"I think your books are great. I love to read them, as does my family."
— *P. C., Milford, MA**

"Your books are some of the best romances I've read."
— *M. B., Zeeland, MI**

"SECOND CHANCE AT LOVE is my favorite line of romance novels."
— *L. B., Springfield, VA**

"I think SECOND CHANCE AT LOVE books are terrific. I married my 'Second Chance' over 15 years ago. I truly believe love is lovelier the second time around!"
— *P. P., Houston, TX**

"I enjoy your books tremendously."
— *I. S., Bayonne, NJ**

"I love your books and read them all the time. Keep them coming—they're just great."
— *G. L., Brookfield, CT**

"SECOND CHANCE AT LOVE books are definitely the best!"
— *D. P., Wabash, IN**

*Name and address available upon request

NEW FROM THE PUBLISHERS OF *SECOND CHANCE AT LOVE!*

To Have and to Hold

___	THEY SAID IT WOULDN'T LAST #4 Elaine Tucker	06931-0
___	THE FAMILY PLAN #7 Nuria Wood	06934-5
___	HOLD FAST 'TIL DAWN #8 Mary Haskell	06935-3
___	HEART FULL OF RAINBOWS #9 Melanie Randolph	06936-1
___	I KNOW MY LOVE #10 Vivian Connolly	06937-X
___	KEYS TO THE HEART #11 Jennifer Rose	06938-8
___	STRANGE BEDFELLOWS #12 Elaine Tucker	06939-6
___	MOMENTS TO SHARE #13 Katherine Granger	06940-X
___	SUNBURST #14 Jeanne Grant	06941-8
___	WHATEVER IT TAKES #15 Cally Hughes	06942-6
___	LADY LAUGHING EYES #16 Lee Damon	06943-4
___	ALL THAT GLITTERS #17 Mary Haskell	06944-2
___	PLAYING FOR KEEPS #18 Elissa Curry	06945-0
___	PASSION'S GLOW #19 Marilyn Brian	06946-9
___	BETWEEN THE SHEETS #20 Tricia Adams	06947-7
___	MOONLIGHT AND MAGNOLIAS #21 Vivian Connolly	06948-5
___	A DELICATE BALANCE #22 Kate Wellington	06949-3
___	KISS ME, CAIT #23 Elissa Curry	07825-5
___	HOMECOMING #24 Ann Cristy	07826-3
___	TREASURE TO SHARE #25 Cally Hughes	07827-1
___	THAT CHAMPAGNE FEELING #26 Claudia Bishop	07828-X
___	KISSES SWEETER THAN WINE #27 Jennifer Rose	07829-8
___	TROUBLE IN PARADISE #28 Jeanne Grant	07830-1
___	HONORABLE INTENTIONS #29 Adrienne Edwards	07831-X
___	PROMISES TO KEEP #30 Vivian Connolly	07832-8
___	CONFIDENTIALLY YOURS #31 Petra Diamond	07833-6
___	UNDER COVER OF NIGHT #32 Jasmine Craig	07834-4
___	NEVER TOO LATE #33 Cally Hughes	07835-2
___	MY DARLING DETECTIVE #34 Hilary Cole	07836-0
___	FORTUNE'S SMILE #35 Cassie Miles	07837-9
___	WHERE THE HEART IS #36 Claudia Bishop	07838-7
___	ANNIVERSARY WALTZ #37 Mary Haskell	07839-5
___	SWEET NOTHINGS #38 Charlotte Hines	07840-9
___	DEEPER THAN DESIRE #39 Jacqueline Topaz	07841-7
___	THE HEART VICTORIOUS #40 Delaney Devers	07842-5

All Titles are $1.95
Prices may be slightly higher in Canada.

Available at your local bookstore or return this form to:

SECOND CHANCE AT LOVE
Book Mailing Service
P.O. Box 690, Rockville Centre, NY 11571

Please send me the titles checked above. I enclose _____ Include 75¢ for postage and handling if one book is ordered; 25¢ per book for two or more not to exceed $1.75. California, Illinois, New York and Tennessee residents please add sales tax.

NAME _____

ADDRESS _____

CITY _____ STATE/ZIP _____

(allow six weeks for delivery)   THTH #67

Second Chance at Love

- ____07812-3 **SOMETIMES A LADY #196** Jocelyn Day
- ____07813-1 **COUNTRY PLEASURES #197** Lauren Fox
- ____07814-X **TOO CLOSE FOR COMFORT #198** Liz Grady
- ____07815-8 **KISSES INCOGNITO #199** Christa Merlin
- ____07816-6 **HEAD OVER HEELS #200** Nicola Andrews
- ____07817-4 **BRIEF ENCHANTMENT #201** Susanna Collins
- ____07818-2 **INTO THE WHIRLWIND #202** Laurel Blake
- ____07819-0 **HEAVEN ON EARTH #203** Mary Haskell
- ____07820-4 **BELOVED ADVERSARY #204** Thea Frederick
- ____07821-2 **SEASWEPT #205** Maureen Norris
- ____07822-0 **WANTON WAYS #206** Katherine Granger
- ____07823-9 **A TEMPTING MAGIC #207** Judith Yates
- ____07956-1 **HEART IN HIDING #208** Francine Rivers
- ____07957-X **DREAMS OF GOLD AND AMBER #209** Robin Lynn
- ____07958-8 **TOUCH OF MOONLIGHT #210** Liz Grady
- ____07959-6 **ONE MORE TOMORROW #211** Aimée Duvall
- ____07960-X **SILKEN LONGINGS #212** Sharon Francis
- ____07961-8 **BLACK LACE AND PEARLS #213** Elissa Curry
- ____08070-5 **SWEET SPLENDOR #214** Diana Mars
- ____08071-3 **BREAKFAST WITH TIFFANY #215** Kate Nevins
- ____08072-1 **PILLOW TALK #216** Lee Williams
- ____08073-X **WINNING WAYS #217** Christina Dair
- ____08074-8 **RULES OF THE GAME #218** Nicola Andrews
- ____08075-6 **ENCORE #219** Carole Buck
- ____08115-9 **SILVER AND SPICE #220** Jeanne Grant
- ____08116-7 **WILDCATTER'S KISS #221** Kelly Adams
- ____08117-5 **MADE IN HEAVEN #222** Linda Raye
- ____08118-3 **MYSTIQUE #223** Ann Cristy
- ____08119-1 **BEWITCHED #224** Linda Barlow
- ____08120-5 **SUDDENLY THE MAGIC #225** Karen Keast

All of the above titles are $1.95
Prices may be slightly higher in Canada.

Available at your local bookstore or return this form to:

SECOND CHANCE AT LOVE
Book Mailing Service
P.O. Box 690, Rockville Centre, NY 11571

Please send me the titles checked above. I enclose _____. Include 75¢ for postage and handling if one book is ordered; 25¢ per book for two or more not to exceed $1.75. California, Illinois, New York and Tennessee residents please add sales tax.

NAME_____

ADDRESS_____

CITY_____ STATE/ZIP_____

(allow six weeks for delivery)   SK-41b